ALREADY

TAKEN

(A Laura Frost Suspense Thriller —Book Six)

BLAKE PIERCE

Blake Pierce

Blake Pierce is the USA Today bestselling author of the RILEY PAGE mystery series, which includes seventeen books. Blake Pierce is also the author of the MACKENZIE WHITE mystery series, comprising fourteen books; of the AVERY BLACK mystery series, comprising six books; of the KERI LOCKE mystery series, comprising five books; of the MAKING OF RILEY PAIGE mystery series, comprising six books; of the KATE WISE mystery series, comprising seven books; of the CHLOE FINE psychological suspense mystery, comprising six books; of the JESSE HUNT psychological suspense thriller series, comprising twenty four books; of the AU PAIR psychological suspense thriller series, comprising three books; of the ZOE PRIME mystery series, comprising six books; of the ADELE SHARP mystery series, comprising fifteen books, of the EUROPEAN VOYAGE cozy mystery series, comprising four books; of the new LAURA FROST FBI suspense thriller, comprising nine books (and counting); of the new ELLA DARK FBI suspense thriller, comprising eleven books (and counting); of the A YEAR IN EUROPE cozy mystery series, comprising nine books, of the AVA GOLD mystery series, comprising six books (and counting); of the RACHEL GIFT mystery series, comprising six books (and counting); of the VALERIE LAW mystery series, comprising six books (and counting); and of the PAIGE KING mystery series, comprising six books (and counting).

An avid reader and lifelong fan of the mystery and thriller genres, Blake loves to hear from you, so please feel free to visit www.blakepierceauthor.com to learn more and stay in touch.

BOOKS BY BLAKE PIERCE

PAIGE KING MYSTERY SERIES
THE GIRL HE PINED (Book #1)
THE GIRL HE CHOSE (Book #2)
THE GIRL HE TOOK (Book #3)
THE GIRL HE WISHED (Book #4)
THE GIRL HE CROWNED (Book #5)
THE GIRL HE WATCHED (Book #6)

VALERIE LAW MYSTERY SERIES
NO MERCY (Book #1)
NO PITY (Book #2)
NO FEAR (Book #3)
NO SLEEP (Book #4)
NO QUARTER (Book #5)
NO CHANCE (Book #6)

RACHEL GIFT MYSTERY SERIES
HER LAST WISH (Book #1)
HER LAST CHANCE (Book #2)
HER LAST HOPE (Book #3)
HER LAST FEAR (Book #4)
HER LAST CHOICE (Book #5)
HER LAST BREATH (Book #6)

AVA GOLD MYSTERY SERIES
CITY OF PREY (Book #1)
CITY OF FEAR (Book #2)
CITY OF BONES (Book #3)
CITY OF GHOSTS (Book #4)
CITY OF DEATH (Book #5)
CITY OF VICE (Book #6)

A YEAR IN EUROPE
A MURDER IN PARIS (Book #1)
DEATH IN FLORENCE (Book #2)

VENGEANCE IN VIENNA (Book #3)
A FATALITY IN SPAIN (Book #4)

ELLA DARK FBI SUSPENSE THRILLER
GIRL, ALONE (Book #1)
GIRL, TAKEN (Book #2)
GIRL, HUNTED (Book #3)
GIRL, SILENCED (Book #4)
GIRL, VANISHED (Book 5)
GIRL ERASED (Book #6)
GIRL, FORSAKEN (Book #7)
GIRL, TRAPPED (Book #8)
GIRL, EXPENDABLE (Book #9)
GIRL, ESCAPED (Book #10)
GIRL, HIS (Book #11)

LAURA FROST FBI SUSPENSE THRILLER
ALREADY GONE (Book #1)
ALREADY SEEN (Book #2)
ALREADY TRAPPED (Book #3)
ALREADY MISSING (Book #4)
ALREADY DEAD (Book #5)
ALREADY TAKEN (Book #6)
ALREADY CHOSEN (Book #7)
ALREADY LOST (Book #8)
ALREADY HIS (Book #9)

EUROPEAN VOYAGE COZY MYSTERY SERIES
MURDER (AND BAKLAVA) (Book #1)
DEATH (AND APPLE STRUDEL) (Book #2)
CRIME (AND LAGER) (Book #3)
MISFORTUNE (AND GOUDA) (Book #4)
CALAMITY (AND A DANISH) (Book #5)
MAYHEM (AND HERRING) (Book #6)

ADELE SHARP MYSTERY SERIES
LEFT TO DIE (Book #1)
LEFT TO RUN (Book #2)
LEFT TO HIDE (Book #3)
LEFT TO KILL (Book #4)
LEFT TO MURDER (Book #5)

LEFT TO ENVY (Book #6)
LEFT TO LAPSE (Book #7)
LEFT TO VANISH (Book #8)
LEFT TO HUNT (Book #9)
LEFT TO FEAR (Book #10)
LEFT TO PREY (Book #11)
LEFT TO LURE (Book #12)
LEFT TO CRAVE (Book #13)
LEFT TO LOATHE (Book #14)
LEFT TO HARM (Book #15)

THE AU PAIR SERIES
ALMOST GONE (Book#1)
ALMOST LOST (Book #2)
ALMOST DEAD (Book #3)

ZOE PRIME MYSTERY SERIES
FACE OF DEATH (Book#1)
FACE OF MURDER (Book #2)
FACE OF FEAR (Book #3)
FACE OF MADNESS (Book #4)
FACE OF FURY (Book #5)
FACE OF DARKNESS (Book #6)

A JESSIE HUNT PSYCHOLOGICAL SUSPENSE SERIES
THE PERFECT WIFE (Book #1)
THE PERFECT BLOCK (Book #2)
THE PERFECT HOUSE (Book #3)
THE PERFECT SMILE (Book #4)
THE PERFECT LIE (Book #5)
THE PERFECT LOOK (Book #6)
THE PERFECT AFFAIR (Book #7)
THE PERFECT ALIBI (Book #8)
THE PERFECT NEIGHBOR (Book #9)
THE PERFECT DISGUISE (Book #10)
THE PERFECT SECRET (Book #11)
THE PERFECT FAÇADE (Book #12)
THE PERFECT IMPRESSION (Book #13)
THE PERFECT DECEIT (Book #14)
THE PERFECT MISTRESS (Book #15)
THE PERFECT IMAGE (Book #16)

THE PERFECT VEIL (Book #17)
THE PERFECT INDISCRETION (Book #18)
THE PERFECT RUMOR (Book #19)
THE PERFECT COUPLE (Book #20)
THE PERFECT MURDER (Book #21)
THE PERFECT HUSBAND (Book #22)
THE PERFECT SCANDAL (Book #23)
THE PERFECT MASK (Book #24)

CHLOE FINE PSYCHOLOGICAL SUSPENSE SERIES
NEXT DOOR (Book #1)
A NEIGHBOR'S LIE (Book #2)
CUL DE SAC (Book #3)
SILENT NEIGHBOR (Book #4)
HOMECOMING (Book #5)
TINTED WINDOWS (Book #6)

KATE WISE MYSTERY SERIES
IF SHE KNEW (Book #1)
IF SHE SAW (Book #2)
IF SHE RAN (Book #3)
IF SHE HID (Book #4)
IF SHE FLED (Book #5)
IF SHE FEARED (Book #6)
IF SHE HEARD (Book #7)

THE MAKING OF RILEY PAIGE SERIES
WATCHING (Book #1)
WAITING (Book #2)
LURING (Book #3)
TAKING (Book #4)
STALKING (Book #5)
KILLING (Book #6)

RILEY PAIGE MYSTERY SERIES
ONCE GONE (Book #1)
ONCE TAKEN (Book #2)
ONCE CRAVED (Book #3)
ONCE LURED (Book #4)
ONCE HUNTED (Book #5)

ONCE PINED (Book #6)
ONCE FORSAKEN (Book #7)
ONCE COLD (Book #8)
ONCE STALKED (Book #9)
ONCE LOST (Book #10)
ONCE BURIED (Book #11)
ONCE BOUND (Book #12)
ONCE TRAPPED (Book #13)
ONCE DORMANT (Book #14)
ONCE SHUNNED (Book #15)
ONCE MISSED (Book #16)
ONCE CHOSEN (Book #17)

MACKENZIE WHITE MYSTERY SERIES
BEFORE HE KILLS (Book #1)
BEFORE HE SEES (Book #2)
BEFORE HE COVETS (Book #3)
BEFORE HE TAKES (Book #4)
BEFORE HE NEEDS (Book #5)
BEFORE HE FEELS (Book #6)
BEFORE HE SINS (Book #7)
BEFORE HE HUNTS (Book #8)
BEFORE HE PREYS (Book #9)
BEFORE HE LONGS (Book #10)
BEFORE HE LAPSES (Book #11)
BEFORE HE ENVIES (Book #12)
BEFORE HE STALKS (Book #13)
BEFORE HE HARMS (Book #14)

AVERY BLACK MYSTERY SERIES
CAUSE TO KILL (Book #1)
CAUSE TO RUN (Book #2)
CAUSE TO HIDE (Book #3)
CAUSE TO FEAR (Book #4)
CAUSE TO SAVE (Book #5)
CAUSE TO DREAD (Book #6)

KERI LOCKE MYSTERY SERIES
A TRACE OF DEATH (Book #1)
A TRACE OF MURDER (Book #2)
A TRACE OF VICE (Book #3)

A TRACE OF CRIME (Book #4)
A TRACE OF HOPE (Book #5)

CHAPTER ONE

Ike was eager to get finished for the day. It had been a long one, with no sign of a rest on the horizon if he didn't get the harvest at least half done. The fields around his family farm had always been big, but every year that went by, Ike was starting to think they were expanding on him. Getting bigger while he slept.

How else could you explain it taking him half as long again to get the harvest in as it had when he was a young man?

He turned the tractor, moving along the next row of corn, checking the sky as he did so. There was a darkening on the edges of the bright blue, a tonal shift signaling the night coming on as the sun headed down into his corn. All those acres of waving golden heads, waiting for him to get to them. Fifteen years ago, he'd have been done already by this late in November.

Fifteen years ago, he wouldn't have felt the ache in his bones as he turned his head to steer the tractor. He cricked his neck, twisting it to the side to try to iron out that kink that just wouldn't go away. Maybe it was the bed. They'd had the mattress how long now? It sunk when Ike's wife climbed in next to him, and—

What was that? A flash of something out in the corn, as he crooked his head from side to side. A disturbance.

A small one, but he looked again and—yes, there it was. An area of broken stalks. They seemed to trail back to the edge of the field, now he saw it.

Goddammit.

Ike switched off the engine, swinging his legs down out of the tractor's cockpit and jumping to the ground. The impact jarred his bones the way it always seemed to lately. He didn't care. He wasn't going to have no damn college kids using his crops as a damn hoax project, making crop circles to put on that FaceTube or whatever they were calling it these days. They looked like they'd only just started. Must not have heard the tractor coming. He stomped through the corn, pushing it aside easily to find the channels between the rows he'd planted himself.

Damn kids were going to get the fear put up them.

1

Up ahead, he could see the place where the stalks broke, the heads disappearing from view. He'd seen it many times over the years. Kids thinking they were funny. This time, he swore to God, they were going to get a swift kick up the rear, and he'd be damned if the Sheriff was going to arrest—

Ike stopped dead, meeting the break in the corn and seeing only one other person in view.

Someone lying facedown on the ground, the stalks trampled and flattened around him.

After a moment, in which the person on the ground did not move, Ike rushed forward. He'd forgotten his anger, discarded immediately when he saw it.

The blood on the stalks.

He awkwardly fell to his knees at the side of the person—a man, he saw now—trying to ignore the old pain in his left knee from when he'd fallen a few years back. Ike reached out, touching the man's shoulder, lifting him just enough so he could see his face.

And swore and fell backwards, almost dislocating his one good hip in the process.

The air felt colder all of a sudden, the cries of the birds flying overhead more ominous. Ike swore again, looking around fast. Whatever happened here, he wanted no part in it.

But it was on his land already, and he'd gotten out of the tractor to take a look. He was out in the open. Exposed.

Ike swore a third time and scrambled to his feet. The corn scratched at his hands as he pushed up, stumbling back through the corn the way he'd come. At least he knew the way. Wasn't going to get lost in the corn like some townie might.

He reached the tractor and hoisted himself up into the seat, slamming the door closed behind him. It wasn't exactly much in the way of protection, but at least the vehicle itself doubled as a weapon.

Catching his breath for a moment, Ike realized he'd seen no one around. The man had been there a long time. He could tell. The blood was dried on the ground. That didn't happen in five minutes.

He was probably safe. Safe enough, at least, to make the call now.

And, Ike thought to himself grimly, if the bastard *was* still out there, at least the Sheriff would know about it when they came to get Ike's body, too.

The line connected on the stupid little cell phone his daughter had made him get a few years back, and Ike waited for the speaker on the other end.

2

"Nine one one, what's your emergency?"

"Best send the Sheriff, Diane," he said, recognizing the voice of the dispatcher. It was a small town, and he'd had to call his fair share of times—for joyride cars and trucks on fire, mostly. "I've got Jamie here lying in my field, throat cut side to side. Looks like they gave him a second smile."

"Well, shit, Ike," Diane said. "I'm sending the Sheriff right away."

CHAPTER TWO

Laura had watched him fall.

The vision had been so strong, and the headache following it so intense. She knew it was happening now. It had to be. It was so strong, there was a chance that she was even too late.

But she couldn't be.

Not for Nate.

She had to save him.

She'd gotten a concussion when the killer in her last case tried to make her one of his victims, sure, and maybe that was making the headache worse—it was hard to tell—but somehow in her gut, Laura knew. He was in danger. The worst kind of danger. And with the intensity of the headache that always followed her visions and gave her a clue about the urgency of what she had seen, she knew she barely had any time to get to him.

But there was one big problem. She couldn't see what he was falling from. The vision hadn't shown her enough to know where he was, and Nate still wasn't answering her calls. There was still time to save him, to push things onto a timeline where the vision she had seen of the future never came to pass.

But only just.

If Division Chief Rondelle didn't answer her call and tell her where Nate was—

"Laura," Rondelle said, his voice crackling through the phone she'd stuck between her left ear and her shoulder, propping it up so she could drive the car. She was heading through the dark streets of D.C. already, toward Nate's place, even if she didn't know whether he was going to be there. It was the only starting point she had, given it was too late at night to expect him at the FBI headquarters.

"Sir," Laura shot back, her voice desperate, "I need to know where Nate is right now!"

There was a pause.

She knew what he was thinking. Nathaniel Lavoie had requested a transfer. He didn't want to be Laura's partner anymore. The tension between them was obvious. Laura had been trying to get in touch with

Nate for weeks, and Rondelle had borne the brunt of a lot of that attempted contact.

It must have sounded to him like she was losing it.

Like she was going to go over and scream at Nate until he cancelled the transfer and agreed to be her partner again, or something worse.

"Laura," Rondelle began, but she didn't let him finish. She knew that tone. She'd heard it from him so many times before. When he was telling her to drop the bone she had and let it go. When he was telling her she wasn't allowed any information about Amy Fallow, the little girl Laura had saved from a homicidally violent father—a ban she'd managed to circumvent anyway. And all the times recently when he'd told her to let Nate go, to stop trying to convince him to stay, to leave him be.

She couldn't let him give her the same speech again. Not now.

Not while Nate's life hung in the balance—literally. She'd seen him falling from a great height, his mouth open in a scream, his arms and legs windmilling uselessly as he tried to save himself.

He wasn't going to make it.

Not unless she could get there and stop him from falling in the first place.

"Sir," Laura snapped, cutting Rondelle off. "This is serious. I have reason to believe there is a threat on Agent Lavoie's life."

Rondelle paused again. "Agent Frost, that is a serious statement. Are you sure about this?"

"SIR!" Laura yelled, unable to take the delay for a moment longer. "His life is at risk—please! Just tell me where he is!"

"Alright," Rondelle replied, his voice taking on new urgency from the other side of the line. "I do know that Agent Lavoie received a strange call about meeting someone at a bridge. He called it in to let me know—thought it was kind of suspicious and wanted it on record. He said he thought it might be one of his informants wanting a chat."

"Which bridge?" Laura demanded, tapping on the screen of her GPS urgently as she attempted to take a corner blind and one-handed. Her tires screeched as she braked hard to avoid a slower car in front, then powered forward around it.

"I'm not sure," Rondelle replied. "He didn't include that detail in the message he left."

"River bridge or traffic bridge?" Laura asked desperately. She tapped the screen again, searching for some kind of landmark that might give her a clue. Something connected to Nate.

She only dimly heard Rondelle express that he still didn't know, over the pounding of the headache, increasing sharply and making her swerve the wheel to the side—

Laura watched Nate backing up against a railing. He was shocked, his hands out in front of him in a gesture of defense, staring at someone behind Laura. Someone she couldn't see. As was usually the case, the vision wouldn't turn, wouldn't show her the one thing she really wanted to see.

Nate's back was against the rails. He shook his head, opening his mouth to say something. Laura couldn't hear it. All she could hear was the screech of the brakes of a train pulling into a station, overpowering Nate's voice completely.

He was desperate. Trying to reason with someone. To make them see sense.

But it didn't work, because in the next moment he was somehow tumbling back over the railing, some great force hitting him in the chest and making him overbalance, his tall height used against him to move his center of gravity over the top tail. He was going over and there was nothing Laura could do to—

Laura groaned with the force of the headache attacking her as the vision cleared. She was used to the momentary interruption, to finding herself back at the wheel of a car. She'd learned how to deal with that a long time ago. But she wasn't ready for the headache, the pain that almost crippled her, making her eyes want to squeeze tightly shut against the light of the sun.

She had to resist. She swerved only momentarily, keeping her car on the road. She checked the map on her GPS and then hit the accelerator, pushing harder.

"Laura? Are you alright?"

Shit. Laura had forgotten she was still on the line with Rondelle. "I'm fine," she said, intending to end the call so she could concentrate on getting to Nate faster.

"I thought I heard a groan of pain," Rondelle pressed.

Laura shook her head impatiently. She couldn't waste time on reassuring him or figuring out a way to explain away everything with a neat ribbon on top. Nate was in danger.

"I know where he is," she said, shortly. "I'm going there now." She cut the call, not bothering to stop and explain how she knew.

The sound of the train had been her first clue. He was above a rail line—not just that, but a station. Then there had been the double rails

6

he was leaning on, with a lower panel of frosted reinforced glass. She'd driven under that overpass enough times to know exactly where it was.

She was less than ten minutes away across the city.

She was going to make it in five.

Laura gunned the accelerator, shooting out around the car in front and then cutting past the car in front of them, earning honked horns and the angry squeal of brakes behind her. She didn't have time to care. Even if she caused an accident, it meant nothing.

She had to save Nate.

"Come on, come on," Laura muttered to herself, hitting the steering wheel in frustration as she pulled up behind slower-moving cars with no room to pass. She needed to get through. No single millisecond of delay was acceptable. She had to get through.

The cars moved, the road clearing as they turned to left and right, and Laura put her foot to the floor again, pushing forward as fast as she could. She would never forgive herself if she couldn't get there in time. She would never forgive herself if Nate went over alone, no one to save him.

For months she'd been having this vision. Not a vision, really—a feeling. A black shadow of death hanging over Nate. She'd tried to keep him out of danger at every possible turn. She'd taken the riskier tasks, tried to make him stay in precincts and cars so he was safe. She'd shied away from his touch, the thing that would trigger that nauseating black aura and cloud her mind until she wanted to throw up. She'd risked their relationship.

In the end, she'd realized that thinking about telling him she was psychic would make the aura of death lessen, so she'd done it. She'd told him.

And it had all been a waste, because now he thought she was crazy, and he was going to die anyway.

Up ahead in the distance, Laura spotted the bridge. Consulting the map for a split second, she spotted the station just to her left. She was almost there. She was almost with him.

She swung the car hard to the left, almost colliding with a taxi that was emerging from the station entrance. Laura ignored the gestures and shouting trailing out of the driver's side window as she left it in her wake, pulling up with a screeching carelessness, letting the car stop where it would stop. There was a staircase leading up to the overpass.

Laura jumped out of the car, leaving it running, the keys still in the ignition. She didn't care. She was an FBI agent. If someone decided to steal her car, she could probably do something about tracking them down. And even if she couldn't—a car was worth far less than her partner of four years, one of the best men she knew, and, by a very long distance, her closest friend.

Laura took the stairs two at a time, racing to the top, the heels she'd been wearing on her date earlier clattering against the metal. She looked to one side and saw him immediately. Nate was easy to spot— six two, well-built, Black, and—the best giveaway of them all— wearing his blue windbreaker with the FBI logo emblazoned on it in yellow.

He was too far away to hear her if she shouted. She could barely even make out his face.

The train appeared on the horizon, as far down the tracks as she could see before buildings got in the way. It was already coming.

Laura took off at full speed, kicking off her shoes as she went.

She yelled his name, but it was useless. He didn't even turn. He was looking at something else—someone else—coming toward him from the other side of the overpass. He had his back to her now, and the other person—a man—was approaching him.

They stood opposite one another. Laura saw it happening as if it were in slow motion. Nate was shaking his head. She screamed his name again, and his gaze flicked in her direction for a moment but then back. She was running at full pelt, not even breathing anymore, not thinking or feeling, just running.

Nate put his hands up in front of him in a gesture of defense, his back hitting the railing as he moved away from the stranger.

No!

Laura forced herself forward faster than she ever had before as Nate shook his head, as his mouth formed an O of surprise, as the stranger standing opposite him stepped forward—

And Laura collided bodily with him, slamming him to the ground, twisting her head and looking up at Nate as she did so. He was teetering, losing his balance—

8

CHAPTER THREE

Laura reached out a hand toward Nate—

He grabbed hold of the rail and held it, pushing himself back to the right posture, staying on the right side of the railing.

He was safe.

Everything seemed to happen at once then, the world coming back to normal speed in a single rush. Laura realized she was lying on top of the man she had tackled sideways, and her hip and shoulder smarted where she'd bowled right into him. He was fighting to get free, probably to go after Nate again. He was shouting something she couldn't understand. The train was screeching by below them, coming to a stop. Her breath came in ragged pants as she tried to recover from the extreme physical exertion it had taken to get here in time. Her head pounded mercilessly.

Nate jumped forward, grabbing the stranger by the wrists and forcing them behind his back as Laura scrambled away. She struggled to breathe, each inhale rasping through a throat that was raw from shouting, tucking her blonde hair back behind her ears as she tried to right herself. The world felt like it was tilting sideways. For a moment she thought she was going to fall off.

Nate clicked a pair of handcuffs on the stranger's wrists. The man was still yelling incoherently, screaming up at the sky as he twisted over his shoulder, still trying to get to Nate. With all his easy strength, Nate held him pinned by those cuffed arms, stopping him from getting up.

"Laura?" Nate said.

She looked at him. It felt as though he was very far away.

"Are you alright?" he asked.

No, she wasn't alright.

But she was. She was because she had done it. She had saved him.

It was over.

Nate pulled a phone out of his pocket, barking instructions into it, calling for backup to take the stranger away. The man had finally stopped yelling, lying still on the ground, his own breathing a furious gasp that came again and again as he rested, having seemingly used up all the fight he had.

"Why are you here?" Nate asked, moving to sit on the ground next to Laura. He kept one leg outstretched, resting it on the stranger's back to keep him still.

"I saw it," Laura said. Her voice scraped against the inside of her throat and rattled against the ringing sides of her skull. "It's what I've been afraid of, all this time. I finally saw it. I came as fast as I could."

Nate stared at her. It was like she could see the pieces moving into place in his mind. As clear as if she'd had a vision from behind his eyes.

"How did you know where to find me?" Nate asked.

"I called Rondelle," Laura said. She put a hand against her own throat, as if that would ease the rawness there. She needed water. "He said you were called out. Didn't know where. I was going to drive all over looking at every bridge in town. But then I saw it again. The railing. Heard the train. Knew where to come."

Nate blinked at her. He looked at the man on the ground. As if knowing that he was in the spotlight again, he gave a desperate shaking, trying to get his arms free and Nate off him and get up. He swore a long string of curses and racial epithets and then gave up.

"Shut up," Nate muttered. He looked at Laura, then at the railing, then back at the man on the ground. "He tried to push me over."

"I saw you falling," Laura said. Her voice cracked. Not just from the screaming. It had been one of the worst things she'd ever seen in her life. There was a top five of hits in her mind: the death of her father from cancer and the shadow of death he'd carried before he was even diagnosed; the death of Amy Fallow, beaten to a pulp by her father, which she had been able to prevent; the case that made her start drinking; the case that made her an alcoholic; and this.

The second time she'd managed to stop someone she cared about deeply from facing a horrible demise.

She'd done it.

It still wasn't sinking in.

Nate was staring at her like she was an alien with three heads. "You... actually saw this in a vision?"

Laura stared at him numbly. If he didn't believe her now, he was never going to. "I told you," she said.

He looked away. The railing. The man on the ground. Back to Laura. It was a circuit, like a pattern his brain had to complete so he could carry on putting all of the pieces together.

"No one else knew where I was," he said. "I didn't tell anyone. I didn't put it into my GPS. I parked at the station and walked up here—you wouldn't have been able to know where I was."

"I saw it," Laura repeated. She felt dull around the edges, like a knife that had been used too many times. Her breathing was back under control, her headache beginning to fade. She thought she had some painkillers in the car maybe.

"It's the only way," Nate was saying, kind of to himself. "Laura…" He reached out slowly. He touched her arm. The bare skin of her wrist. She wanted to flinch away, unwilling to see the shadow of death again.

But there was nothing.

Only peace.

"You saw this in a vision," he said.

It wasn't a question. From the tone of his voice, Laura knew that he at last understood. He at last believed her.

"All it took was saving your life again, huh?" Laura said, feeling like she was coming back into herself a little, seeing the humor in it.

"Yeah," Nate said distantly, then looked back at her sharply. "Again?"

Laura gave a weary chuckle. Oh, if he only knew the number of times she'd done something stupid to try and stop him from being in danger.

Nate looked off into the distance, then back at her. The stranger on the ground had stopped trying to resist. He was lying looking up at the sky, like he knew he was looking at it for the last time.

"You know him?" Laura asked, nodding in his direction.

Nate nodded. "Arrested him about five years ago on a drugs charge. Before I was partnered with you. He just got out of prison, said he had some information for me."

"Wanted you dead," the man muttered, his voice finally low and slow enough that Laura could understand it. "You ruined my life."

"No, buddy, that was all you," Nate said, shaking his head. Below them, sirens were coming closer, racing toward where they were. Backup.

"He would have done it," Laura said. It probably wasn't necessary. Nate had felt the lightest part of that shove, the part that Laura hadn't quite defused. He must know the rest.

There was a pause, a moment of silence between the three of them. The rest of the city was noisy enough. Another train was coming in. The sirens reached a crescendo below and then shut off as the cars stopped.

11

Laura looked at Nate. He was looking back at her but quickly glanced away. There was something in his face... something that stung.

"Nate?" she said.

"Uh, yeah," he said. He scrambled to his feet, dusting himself off. He loomed over the man who had tried to kill him, reluctant to leave his side but also very obviously eager to get away from Laura. "I'd better make sure they take him in and get all the details right."

"Nate," she said again. He had to see that she was still the same person she'd always been. He hadn't known, and then he hadn't believed—but all the years they'd been working together, she'd been this way under the surface.

"I believe you," he said. There was an urgency in his voice, like he needed her to listen. He needed it so he could end the conversation and get away. So that he didn't have to be around her anymore. "I do. I just... wow, Laura. This is a lot."

"I know," Laura said. That numbness was falling over her again. Didn't he think she knew? She'd had to live with this curse for her whole life.

"I have to go," Nate said, starting a few steps in the direction of the cops now coming across the overpass toward them. Then he hesitated, looking back at the ground. He wanted to run so badly. Laura could see it. It was only duty holding him back.

"I'll go," Laura said instead, standing up. "They know where to reach me if they want a statement." She turned to leave, walking in the opposite direction from where the cops were coming from even though it would mean a longer trip back to her car.

"Laura," Nate called.

She turned and looked at him.

"Thanks," he said. "For saving my life."

Laura nodded, then continued walking.

Her partner of several years, her closest friend, and now the only one who knew her secret.

And he couldn't even stand to be around her.

CHAPTER FOUR

Laura looked up from the steering wheel to see a familiar view in front of her, one she hadn't even realized was going to be there. She'd driven on autopilot. She didn't even remember getting back into the car, setting off, or driving here.

She must have known she needed support, and taken herself subconsciously to the one place she knew she was likely to get it.

It felt strange, coming here without Lacey, her daughter. Lacey and Amy had become such good friends ever since Amy was adopted by her uncle, Christopher Fallow. Their playdates had started as an excuse for Laura to check up on Chris, make sure that he was a good person. She'd saved Amy's life twice—once from kidnappers who thought the governor was a good target for ransom, and once from the homicidally violent governor himself. But once Governor Fallow had gone to prison, Laura hadn't been able to let the case go. She didn't want to wake up one day and find that yet another person who was supposed to look after Amy's life had finally ended it.

That was how it had started off. Now…

She found herself in front of the house, walking on autopilot still, knocking on the door before she could even think about whether this was a good idea.

"Hey," Christopher said, opening the door with one hand while putting a dishcloth over his shoulder with the other. He looked downward as if expecting to see Lacey, then back up at Laura again. At the same moment, she realized she was still wearing the dress she'd had on for their date a few hours earlier. She hadn't gone back for the shoes, too dazed to think about it. She'd put on some boots she found in her trunk to drive. He, meanwhile, was still in that smart shirt, the sleeves rolled up now, his brown hair just a little mussed from whatever he'd been doing since he got home.

Maybe this had been a mistake.

"Um," Laura said. She wasn't really sure how this was supposed to go. She hadn't dated since breaking up with her ex-husband, Marcus, and this thing with Chris was new. Incredibly new. In fact, she still wasn't really sure that it was anything, only that she wanted it to be.

A frown of concern fell over Chris's face. "Are you alright?" he asked. When she didn't immediately answer, still flustered and fumbling for a response, he stepped aside and beckoned. "You'd better come in."

Laura glanced around as she entered; the house was unusually quiet. Chris led her into the kitchen, switching on the hall lights as they passed through. "Amy?" she asked, only able to formulate one-word thoughts for the moment that weren't crippling anxiety about having made the wrong choice by coming here.

"She's sleeping over at a friend's house," Chris said, getting a couple of mugs out of a cupboard and switching on his coffee machine. He clearly could tell that she needed it. "I thought it would be better that way, just in case our date ran later than I expected."

Laura winced, sitting down on a stool at the kitchen island. Her feet hurt from running barefoot across the overpass and walking back to her car afterwards. Her head was still pounding despite the painkillers she'd taken. She briefly considered asking Chris for something stronger, since he was a doctor—but she discarded the thought immediately. As a recovering alcoholic, strong drugs that might take away her inhibitions or leave her groggy were a very bad idea.

"I take it the end of our date wasn't the end of your night," Chris said. He was matter-of-fact about it, not jealous or judgmental. He set a steaming mug of coffee in front of her, which she wrapped her fingers around gratefully.

The warmth reminded her that she'd been cold, too, out there. She shivered a little. "I had to go after Nate," she said. "Nathaniel, my partner. Ex-partner. My point is, we've worked together a long time."

A flicker of a smile passed over Chris's face. "Sounds complicated."

"To say the least," Laura said, then shook her head to clear it. "We had a fight recently. A few months back. He never got over it, requested a transfer. But we've been friends and partners for years, so I've been trying to convince him to let me back in. It was... a stupid fight."

She was leaving out a lot, she knew. She had to. She'd never told anyone about her abilities until very recently. The first, a relative stranger who served as a tester, freaked out and acted like she must have been making it all up. The second had been Nate. He'd swung from disbelieving to not wanting to be around her pretty fast.

There was no way she could handle that kind of rejection twice in one night. Chris was a nice guy, but Laura wasn't going to take the risk.

"So, you went after him tonight to try and convince him to stay?" Chris asked, sipping at his coffee. Laura took his cue and did the same. It was too hot, but it made her feel better almost instantly.

"No," Laura said, then realized immediately it was a good cover story for the truth and backtracked. "Well, yes, but that's not what happened. When I found him, on a bridge over the rail tracks, he was with someone he'd arrested years ago. The criminal managed to lure him there by pretending he had insider information from his time in prison. He actually wanted to kill him. I got there just in time to stop him from pushing Nate over the edge."

"How did you stop him?" Chris asked, his eyes wide. He glanced down at her dress, and Laura did the same to realize she'd managed to dirty it up pretty well when she made her desperate tackle.

"I launched myself at him and tackled him to the ground," she admitted.

"Jesus!" Chris exclaimed. "Are you alright? Any injuries?"

"No, no," Laura said, waving him away. "I'm fine. I just used up a lot of energy and gave myself a headache."

Chris nodded in understanding. "Wow. That sounds like a lot. Hopefully the coffee will help—after this, I'll get you a water so you can rehydrate. How about a snack? Some fruit, maybe?"

Laura couldn't prevent a smile from slipping onto her face. So this was what it was like to date a doctor. "I'll be fine, Dr. Fallow," she said.

Chris made a sheepish face. "Can't help it," he said. "It's a reflex. All those years of training, you know?"

Laura smiled deeper and shook her head. "I'm not complaining. Not really. It's... nice. To have someone care."

Something softened in Chris's expression, his brown eyes flicking over her with sympathy in that assessing way that he had. That was probably a doctor thing, too. She couldn't understand, now, how she'd ever thought that there was a risk of him being anything like his brother. Though they shared some similarities in their looks, their manners and behaviors couldn't have been more different. "If you refuse my official advice to eat some fruit, then can I at least interest you in a slice of cake?"

Laura pretended to think about it. "Hmm. I bet it would be good for my blood sugar."

Chris rolled his eyes and laughed. "I hope you like carrot cake. That's all we have."

15

"Good enough for me." Laura shrugged. She wasn't really hungry after the meal they'd eaten together earlier, but she wasn't joking about the blood sugar. The cake probably would help her to balance out a bit.

Chris clattered around his kitchen, bringing out two plates and then unearthing a cake from underneath a dome, taking out two slices. "I got this from Amy's favorite café," he said. "Better not tell her we ate them without her. I might have to pretend it was fairies."

"Cake fairies?" Laura chuckled.

"They're vicious little things," Chris said, handing her the plate and a fork. "We're lucky we didn't see them. They might have taken our eyes out."

Laura made a horrified face. "Maybe don't tell that part to Amy."

Chris laughed heartily. "No, maybe not."

Laura sighed, a deep breath in and out. She was feeling better already. Yes, her feet still hurt and her head still ached, but she was warm, with all the hydration and nourishment she needed, and Chris was good company. Sympathetic, kind, caring. Exactly the kind of person you leaned on when you needed someone.

She hoped this wasn't a sign that she was getting in too deep, too soon.

"So, how did you leave things with Nate?" Chris asked, taking a bite of his cake. "Are you on good terms again now you've saved his life?"

Laura sighed and shook her head. "He thanked me. But... I don't think he's going to want to see me for a while. He's still processing everything."

"Processing?" Chris frowned. "What's there to process about a fight? Can't he just... accept that you disagree and move on?"

Ah. Laura had gotten herself into a muddle with the story she'd told him and the truth. "I guess he always thought we shared the same views," she said, internally complimenting herself on a good save. "Now that he can see we're different after all, I guess it was a shock. I don't think he's angry anymore, really. Just... dealing with it."

Chris nodded sagely. "Then you'll be partners again before you know it."

A ghost of a smile flitted across Laura's face. "I hope you're right," she said.

Her watch buzzed on her wrist, making her jump. An incoming call. Where had she even put her cell? Laura cast around for a moment only to discover that she had brought her purse in with her, something she

16

didn't remember doing, and that it was on the floor. She hopped down from the stool at the island and pulled it out, groaning at the caller ID.

Rondelle.

She'd never called him back to let him know what had happened. He was probably wondering what on earth that call had been about earlier.

"Sorry," she said to Chris, then pressed the answer button, retreating into the hall. "Chief."

"Agent Frost," Rondelle said. "I gather you were involved in Agent Lavoie's little fracas earlier. I've got a report on my desk saying you haven't yet given a witness statement."

"Right," Laura said. Paperwork? That was why he was calling her so late in the evening? She had often suspected that Rondelle didn't actually sleep. For the man to be as on-call as he was, he surely had to be a robot disguised as a human. "Can I make a statement in the morning? Tonight was... a lot."

"I doubt that would be possible," Rondelle replied. "Since I'm booking you onto a flight in a couple of hours to go to your next case."

Laura blinked. She looked down at her own hand, still lightly bandaged. She'd burned it while confronting the killer in her last case, fighting for her life so that she wouldn't become his next victim. She'd been put on a week of leave afterwards—and, yes, that week was up tomorrow, but she hadn't been expecting to jump right in immediately. She'd thought maybe a week or two of desk duty, paperwork from all the cases she'd fallen behind on, maybe some mandatory counseling if she was unlucky.

Not right on a plane to another case.

"Sir," she said, trying to think of a way to point all of this out.

"I know you're only just back off leave, but we need you on this one," Rondelle said. "Lavoie is still on a leave of absence, as you know, so I can't put him on it. I've sent out half my staff to a terrorism case in Texas, that mass shooter I'm sure you've been hearing about while you've been on your week of rest. All I have left are rookies—and you."

"Great," Laura sighed. "So I'm your last resort." She ran a hand back over the top of her blonde hair, wishing she hadn't tied it up in a ponytail so she could pull at the strands. Today was proving to be very stressful, after what had been an incredibly promising start.

"Not exactly," Rondelle grunted. His voice got even gruffer than usual. "I do value your work, Laura. You're one of my best, you know that. And this has all the hallmarks of being one of those cases that you excel at."

Laura considered this. "You mean it looks like a difficult case to solve."

"Correct," Rondelle replied, a hint of laughter just hiding behind his voice. "That's why I need you. Look, you can tell me you're not ready, and I'll find someone else—but I would appreciate it if you didn't. If you can get here now, I'll brief you on the case. I'm sending you with a partner, just so you don't complain at me when you get here."

Laura groaned. "Agent Won again?" she asked, naming the kid she'd ended up stuck with last time. It had been a lot of hard work, but she'd almost gotten him housebroken. Maybe it wouldn't be so bad to work with him again—though she meant that only grudgingly.

"No, he's still on leave with his injuries, too," Rondelle replied cheerfully. "I have someone new for you. You'll like her. See you within the hour, Agent."

He hung up.

Laura stared at the phone, shaking her head wordlessly. He was putting her with someone new, on a difficult case, on the day she was back from leave—with her hand still bandaged—and right after she'd had to save the life of her ex-partner, who was also still not really talking to her.

This day just couldn't get any better.

"Do you need to go?" Chris asked. He was hovering in the doorway to the kitchen, looking as though he hadn't wanted to eavesdrop but had heard every word.

Laura sighed. "Yeah," she said. She rubbed her eyes. "I've got to head out on a new assignment."

"Now?" Chris stepped closer, taking hold of her hand. He examined the bandage, turning it as if he could see the wound through it. "Surely you need more leave time!"

"There's no one else," Laura sighed.

And it was true, in more ways than one. Even if there was another agent available, they wouldn't be able to do what she could do.

They wouldn't be able to solve the murders with mystical psychic visions that would lead her right to the killer without needing traditional clues or waiting for the murderer to mess up.

No matter what happened to her, how low she felt like she was sinking, Laura would always carry that burden. There was no one else out there who could do what she did. She'd wasted a lot of time looking for them, and she had to admit it to herself: she was the only one.

If she didn't step up, more people could die unnecessarily.

"I'll see you when I get back?" she said, pulling her hand free of Chris's grip. If she let him hold it any longer, she might end up never leaving. "I don't know if it will be in time for Saturday."

"We'll play it by ear," Chris said. He smiled, but it was full of concern.

There was no one else.

Laura nodded, took a breath, and turned to leave his house and head for her car.

CHAPTER FIVE

Laura stepped into Rondelle's office instead of waiting. The door had been left open, and she could see him sitting behind his desk—and standing in front of it, a young woman she didn't recognize.

It didn't take being the best FBI agent in the whole Bureau to figure out who that had to be. Laura's new so-called partner. She wondered how long this one was going to last.

"Ah, Agent Frost," Rondelle said. There was a slight tinge of relief to his voice. That was odd.

"Oh, Agent Frost!" the young woman repeated, with considerably more enthusiasm. She spun around to look at Laura, her auburn hair whipping around in the air behind her in a ponytail not unlike Laura's own. "It's so nice to meet you!"

Laura looked at Rondelle for help as the new agent reached out to vigorously shake her hand. Aha. She was beginning to get an idea of why he looked like he also needed rescuing. "Who am I meeting?"

"Oh!" the agent exclaimed. She had blue eyes that had something about them Laura couldn't quite define. Too wide and too narrow at the same time. If she'd met her on a case, Laura would probably have been wondering if she was a suspect. "I'm Bee Moore. Agent Moore, I mean!"

Too familiar. Laura needed to get this girl to turn the volume down a notch before they even started. She gritted her teeth at what felt like a joke instead of a name, too. Instead of facing Rondelle for the briefing, she squared off against her new partner. Bee was younger than her, clearly a new graduate in her early twenties. There was a light smattering of freckles across her nose and cheeks that made her look even younger. "What is Bee short for? Beatrice?" she asked. She wasn't going to be calling her partner by any nickname.

"Bee is my full name." Agent Moore beamed. "I was raised on a commune."

"Okay," Laura said, looking back over at Rondelle. Apparently, Moore was expecting something more, because she was still watching Laura with what she could see from the corner of her eye was an almost manic grin. "Great."

Rondelle was trying unsuccessfully to hide a smile.

20

"I've heard so much about you," Agent Moore gushed. "You're, like, the best agent out there, right? I mean, the best woman agent, anyway. On our first day out of training, we got to see how many cases all of the agents have worked on, and you've done so many!"

"I'm about a decade older than you," Laura said. She felt too tired for this conversation. Her head was beginning to pound harder again. "You'll have time to catch up."

"Right, of course," Moore said. "And you must tell me—"

"Was there a briefing?" Laura asked, cutting Moore off before she could fry Laura's head even further with her over-the-top eagerness. She felt a little guilty, though, and tried to soften it. "I just figure we should hear the briefing, then get going. We can get to know each other on the way."

That was a lie—or so she hoped. If this perky little agent didn't allow her to sleep on the plane to wherever they were going, there might be more than one body to deal with when they arrived.

"Yes," Rondelle said, leaning forward with the case notes in a slim folder. Laura stepped closer to take them, as she always liked to. Whoever held the case notes could determine when they talked about the case, and she didn't want to do a whole lot of that until they were already on the ground. "I'm sending you to a small town a little out of Dayton, Ohio."

Laura's heart sank. That was, what, an hour and a half flight? No time to rest. They'd have to hit the ground running as soon as they got there.

"Laura, I'm aware that you need to take it easy," Rondelle said, a little gruffly. "Agent Moore, one of your jobs will be to enforce that. Starting with this directive: once you land, I want you to go straight to your hotel. There's only one in the town—I'm afraid it's a little old inn, but I'm sure you'll find it comfortable. I've asked them to stay open to allow you late entrance since you'll be there after midnight, and they were happy to oblige. Check in, sleep, and report to the local sheriff in the morning, not before. Got that?"

Laura's shoulders slumped—not because she was disagreeing with the order, but out of relief. "Got it."

"That'll get you fresh on the case when you head in," Rondelle said. He tipped his head to the side slightly as if considering. "Also, the tickets are cheaper late at night than early in the morning."

"Glad to know you have our best interests at heart," Laura said, with a small smile. Then she regretted it; to the side, she noticed Agent Moore staring at her with an open-mouthed admiration. No doubt, she

21

was in awe of how Laura could get away with being irreverent in front of the boss.

It didn't hurt that they'd been through a lot. When Laura had tried again and again to save Amy Fallow from her abusive father's clutches, it had been Rondelle who had to stand up for her in front of the head of their whole organization.

He hadn't asked her about the thing with Nate. Laura had a feeling he was done with all the drama, and wanted her to get out of the state quickly so that everything had time to cool down. It wasn't as though they needed much of a new witness statement—Nate's word and the surveillance footage from the overpass would cover much of it.

"This case is not a laughing matter," Rondelle said, sobering the mood in the room instantly. "We've just had a second body found earlier today. Within such a small town, one murder is quite uncommon and I gather this is the first such death that the Sheriff's team has dealt with in over fifteen years. The second murder officially puts this out of their depth. It's a grisly one, too. I recommend you take a look at the photographs."

Laura obediently opened up the file and took the first printout—a series of reproduced crime scene photographs on normal printer paper. Not what they would be working with when they landed, but enough to give them an idea for now.

And what an idea.

There were two different bodies, but the injuries on them were similar. One of them was lying in what looked like a cornfield, with a gaping wound across the throat which had spilled blood in a wide swathe around it. The other was easier to see and study: this one was lying on its back, and it was possible to make out the devastation that had been wrought across the torso.

It was ripped to pieces, slashed over and over again with some kind of blade. There was a lot of fury and violence in those slashes. It was clearly far from the average murder.

There was something going on here, and it was not at all pretty.

"Oh, gosh," Agent Moore gasped, shaking her head and covering her mouth with one hand. She looked like she was about to start crying.

Laura was glad Rondelle had suggested they look at the pictures now. Having that reaction when they were in front of the local sheriffs in Ohio would have been embarrassing. It was just about as much of a cliché as the rookie throwing up at their first body.

22

"Both local residents?" Laura asked, flipping away from the gruesome photographs and over to the rest of the file, which contained the basic information on the case as it was known so far.

"Yes, they have both been identified," Rondelle said. "I think you can see where this is going. With two bodies showing up in as many days, this has the makings of a spree killer—or even a serial killer. You need to get down there and catch him before it goes that far."

Laura was studying a little further down the first page. "Left in broad daylight, too," she mused. "This could get interesting. He's not shy at all, is he?"

"No, he is not," Rondelle agreed. Moore was still looking between them with a tragic expression on her face, as if she thought that they were being too blasé in the face of all of these terrible details.

"You'll get used to it, kid," Laura said. She pushed the file into Moore's hands, changing her mind about holding onto it. With any luck, it would horrify the rookie so much she wouldn't want to discuss anything at all. "We'd better get going. How long until the flight?"

"Half an hour," Rondelle said, checking his watch.

Moore made a squeaking noise. "I don't have anything packed yet," she said, clutching the file against her chest as if it was going to save her.

"Oh dear," Laura said dryly. Maybe she would have had more sympathy if she wasn't tired, aching, still supposed to be on leave but being emotionally blackmailed by her direct superior, and desperate for a drink she wasn't allowed to have. "I suppose you'd better rush, then."

"But I live outside of the city," Moore said, her voice rising almost to a wail.

"Maybe you two should get on different flights," Rondelle suggested with a heavy sigh. "I can push yours back a little, Agent Moore. Next time, I expect you to be prepared. Always carry a bug-out bag in your car so you're ready to go if I need to send you directly from the briefing."

"Yes, sir," Moore said, her voice faint as if she was completely disappointed in herself.

Laura started walking out of the office, inwardly thanking whatever gods were looking out for her for the chance to really get some rest without an annoying newbie partner at her side. She was going to get an hour's sleep on the flight, get to this inn or whatever it was, and sleep for the rest of the night—and nothing was going to interrupt her until dawn.

Then, this killer had better watch his back—because she wasn't in a mood to be taking any prisoners.

CHAPTER SIX

Laura blinked into the mirror behind the driver's side sun visor, rubbing at the corner of her eye. There was still some gritty sleep there, and it dislodged under her finger, leaving her feeling much better. Not that it made much overall difference. She was still tired as hell.

Thankfully, she was back to normal levels of tired after half a night's sleep in the cramped and uncomfortably cozy inn, which had so many different handmade rustic blankets on the bed Laura had ended up pushing them all onto the floor. Still, she had to admit, she'd had a marginally better sleep than she did in the usual rock-hard creaking motel beds they got stuck in. That was one of the things you learned quickly as an FBI agent on assignment: how to sleep anywhere, anytime, at a moment's notice.

"The lights are changing," Agent Bee Moore chirped up from the passenger side.

Laura snapped the sun visor back up into position, putting her foot back on the accelerator and crossing the intersection. She made no comment—she was sure she would have realized it was time to move when the other car in front of them did. Agent Moore was already far too cheerful and eager for this time of the morning, sleep or no sleep.

Laura had found her waiting outside of her own door, hanging about on the inn's upstairs landing, when she emerged to head for the sheriff's office. Apparently, she was very keen to demonstrate that her lateness last night was not going to be a habit.

"Sheriff's office sent us the direct coordinates of the most recent victim. It's a farm outside town," Laura said. The first thing she'd said to Moore since suggesting they go get in the rental car. The town was small enough that they could have walked to see the Sheriff if they were just meeting him there. "We'll head out there and check out the crime scene first, then to the morgue to look at the bodies."

"What's the Sheriff's name? Will it just be him we're meeting?" Moore asked. She dug a notebook and pen out of her coat pocket.

"Sheriff Ramsgate, and I don't know," Laura told her. She squinted ahead, checking the route against the GPS. They were already heading out of town. It would only take them ten or fifteen minutes to get to the scene, depending on how good the roads were.

"Okay. Is he in charge of the crime scene? Or are we, now? Do we have to make sure it doesn't get disturbed?"

Laura glanced at her. "They didn't cover all of this in training?"

Moore flushed slightly. "They did, but it was a lot to take in," she said. "Besides, I figure being out here on assignment is probably nothing like what they say it is in training, right?"

That much was true, Laura had to admit. "Not in that sense," she said. "Chain of command is kind of set into the procedures. We're in charge of everything, but we can usually trust the locals to do an okay job. If I see anything that doesn't look up to scratch, like civilians wandering around or failure to protect the integrity of the scene, then I'll step up and give out orders. But we won't have to do that ourselves. We can ask the Sheriff's staff to do it, and if he doesn't have enough, then we draft in reinforcements."

"Got it," Moore said, scratching something down in her notebook. Laura hoped it wasn't verbatim. She'd expected the rookie to be green, but not that green. "So, you've been with the FBI a long time, right?"

Laura blinked. She wasn't *that* old, was she? "Just about nine years now."

"Wow," Moore said. "I hope I'm here for that long! And you have such a great record, too. What's your secret?"

Laura's nostrils flared. Just how young was this kid, anyway? She was aware that nine years probably did sound like a long time for someone who'd never committed to anything longer than a high school, but still. All these questions.

"I don't have a secret," she said. "I've just done the job enough times to know how to do the job."

Alright, so that wasn't entirely fair. She actually did have a secret. There was just no question at all that Laura was going to share it. There wasn't even any point, since it wasn't as though Agent Moore could use the same technique.

"You must have picked up some tips and tricks along the way," Agent Moore pressed. "Like, I don't know. What's the first thing we should be looking for at the crime scene?"

"Evidence," Laura said, then thought about it and corrected herself. "No—a body. Look for a body first and then evidence."

Moore made a pouty kind of sound and looked out the passenger window. Laura was glad. She didn't want to answer all of these stupid questions. She'd had enough to deal with on her last case with Agent Won, who thought he knew everything and didn't need her help at all.

26

Now she was paired up with someone who wanted her hand held every step of the way. It was like Rondelle was playing a trick on her.

"They said you were tough to work with, too," Moore said, almost to herself. "I just thought it was probably because they didn't like the fact a woman was better at the job than they were."

There was a note in her voice that made Laura flick her eyes sideways, getting an impression of the side of Moore's face before she looked back at the road ahead. They were winding through fields now. Not far from the flag marking the spot on the GPS.

Damn. The rookie actually looked up to her, didn't she?

She was looking for some kind of role model to guide her through the Bureau.

Unfortunately, that just wasn't something that Laura had the time or the headspace to be. She'd have to think of a way to break it to her gently. Or, failing that, just be her usual prickly and tough to work with self until the girl gave up and started idolizing someone else.

"I think this is it," Laura said, choosing not to make any comment about what Agent Moore had said. The less dialogue they entered on that part, the better. Even if it wasn't her favorite thing about the job, Laura had long ago made peace with the fact that everyone else in the FBI, other than Nate, thought she was a freak or a snobbish bitch.

She'd made peace with it through the medium of alcohol, which was no longer an option, but that was beside the point.

They turned off onto a dirt track which led past a few rickety-looking outbuildings before plunging through the field of corn. Off to one side it was possible to see that half the field had been cleared. The rest was still waiting, golden ears waving in the slight breeze, putting Laura in mind of every bad horror movie from the last thirty years. She shuddered slightly, then pushed it out of her head

This wasn't even her first crime scene in a field of corn. But even if the crop's reputation for spookiness *was* justified, there wasn't any killer out there today. Not with the Sheriff parked outside a large and welcoming farmhouse that appeared as if rising out of the field itself, along with several trucks and heavier farm vehicles left in neat rows in front.

Laura pulled up beside them all, switching off the engine and glancing in the rearview mirror just once before getting out.

"Where is everyone?" Agent Moore wondered out loud, getting out at the same time.

Laura turned in a circle, then pointed. There was a clear disturbance in the wall of corn that faced them on the left-hand side of the track they'd driven down. "I'm guessing we go that way."

The walk through the corn was eerie. Each time the wind brushed through the stalks, they shivered against one another and made a sound not a million miles away from whispering. Laura was confident, though, that they were in the right place—and when the view changed from an indiscriminate passageway through identical stalks of corn into an open clearing where two men were standing, looking down at the ground and talking in quiet voices, Laura knew she'd been right.

The biggest clue was the fact that one of them was the Sheriff, given his brown uniform.

"Hi," Laura said, grabbing her badge off her belt to wave it at them. "We just arrived. I'm Special Agent Laura Frost, and this is my partner, Special Agent Bee Moore."

"Be more what?" the Sheriff asked. He was an older man, probably in his fifties, with graying hair at the sides of a dark short-cropped cut. He had a small paunch right where his belt sat, and he was standing with his thumbs hooked under the belt as if to ease the pressure. He looked like probably more than half of all the sheriffs that Laura had ever met. She guessed the job took a certain type.

Laura wanted to wince at the pun he'd made of Moore's name, but when she turned to look to her side, the rookie was grinning. "Anything I want," she said. "My parents wanted me to know I could always just 'be more.'"

Huh. Apparently, she was serious—and she didn't even look angry about it.

"Sheriff Ramsgate, I'm guessing?" Laura asked, trying to get the conversation back on track. She was sure that Agent Moore had a very interesting backstory, from the small snippet she'd already heard. But Laura had already expended enough energy on the last partner who only stuck around for one case. If Agent Moore came back for a second, then maybe she would find the time to try to care.

"That's right," the Sheriff said, reaching up to touch the brim of his hat almost as a kind of reflex. "This here is Ike Brown, the owner of the property. He's also the one who found the body and called it in."

Laura nodded, turning her attention to the ground before them. There was a section which had been trampled down close around where they stood, and quite clearly an actual crime scene which started after that. Someone from the Sheriff's team, quite possibly the man himself, had erected a small scrap of tape between two metal spikes in front of

28

the blood-spattered area, as if protecting an exhibit at a museum. "This is where the body was found?"

"Yes, ma'am," Ike spoke up. "I found it last night. We had a clear night, no rain, so it's all intact."

Laura was already nodding. "This cordon is nowhere near good enough," she said. "Sheriff, I'm going to need this whole section of field protected. We've probably lost a lot of potential forensic evidence already, but we'll do what we can to save it. Come on—none of us should be this close to the site right now, given that it hasn't been properly processed."

Sheriff Ramsgate bristled as she turned. She could see it in him. Righteous indignation. He thought he knew how to do his job. The trouble was, she was already well aware that he hadn't dealt with a crime on this scale before.

"Tell me about the victim," she continued, starting to lead him away. The best way to do it was just to cut him off, get him talking about something else, so he wouldn't have the time to voice his anger. He was just going to have to deal with being given orders. Most sheriffs weren't used to it—usually being the ones giving the orders—but he was the one who needed the help of the FBI, so he was going to have to accept the form that it came in.

"He's a local man, James Bluton," Ramsgate said after a moment, falling into step behind her as Laura had known he would have to. Behind him, Ike and Agent Moore brought up the back of the party, following them out of the channel through the corn. "He's in his thirties. A family man. His wife was out of town visiting family, but we've notified her and she's on her way back here now."

"How far away?" Laura asked.

"What?"

"The wife."

"Oh—more than a few hours," Ramsgate said, making a shrugging gesture. "I'm not real sure on the location. Just know it was far enough she decided to stay there a few days instead of traveling right back."

Laura nodded. They would have to get someone to follow that up. Speak to the relatives and make sure the wife had been there the whole time. It was so often something to do with the spouse. Even though violent murders of this nature were very rarely committed by women, they had to be sure.

"What was he like?" Laura asked. "It's a small town—I guess you probably knew him."

Ramsgate nodded out of the corner of her eye as they emerged back onto the dirt track that they had driven in on. Out in front of the farmhouse, a woman who looked to be about Ike's age—probably in her sixties or so—was setting out what looked like a pot of tea and some empty mugs on a table on the porch. "I knew him to see around," Sheriff Ramsgate said. "He owns the farm on the adjacent land here. Ike's the one who knew him better."

Ike nodded when Laura looked at him over her shoulder. He was pale-faced, like he still wasn't over the discovery. She didn't blame him. This was the one that had been facedown—she'd been able to tell from the blood spilled over the earth and the trampled corn stalks at the scene. He'd only seen the cut throat. But that, she was sure, would easily have been enough.

"Alright, Ike," Laura said, taking the cue from the Sheriff and using his first name. "Here's what we're going to do. We'll sit down on that porch of yours—that's your wife, is it?"

Ike nodded. "Yes, ma'am, that's my Pat."

"Right, we'll sit down, drink some of Pat's tea, and then talk about Mr. Bluton," she said. As she glanced over to get his confirmation, she noticed Agent Moore staring at her excitedly. She had the kind of expression that said she was finally getting to see the master in action. Laura suppressed a groan.

They seated themselves around a square table on garden chairs that were weather-beaten, the wood bleached with time and marked with old stains. Laura accepted the cup of tea from Pat Brown when she poured it, happy to at least get something warm inside of her. The weather was cold, and while it wasn't freezing yet, the FBI windbreakers they wore were never quite enough against real winter climes.

Ike and the Sheriff barely seemed affected by it, but Laura waited until everyone had their hands wrapped around a warm mug of tea— Agent Moore included—before she started. Time was of the essence here, but there was nothing to be gained by rushing and alienating a key witness.

"So, tell me about Mr. Bluton. What was he like?" Laura asked.

Ike shrugged, looking down into his tea with a frown. "Not a bad guy," he said. "Kept his head down and worked. With a young family like that, only taking over the farm from his folks a few years back, he had a lot of work to do."

"He'd been around here his whole life?"

"More or less." Ike shrugged again. "Went off to college a few years, to get some advanced farming techniques or some such. Didn't make him stuck up about it, though. Just mostly used the same methods as his daddy in the end."

"You say he's a neighbor," Laura said, taking a map of the local area out of her pocket. They'd been on sale at the reception of the inn she was staying at, and it had seemed useful. "Can you mark out his land for me?" She was about to reach into her pocket for a pen, but Agent Moore beat her to it, clicking the nib out rapidly and practically shooting it into Ike's hand.

Ike took the paper with the rough approach of a lifelong manual laborer, his hands unused to holding a pen. "It's this whole field here," he said, sketching it out with short, unpracticed strokes. "You see? Goes right the way across to the highway. His home's 'round about here."

Laura studied the markings he had made. "So, then, how did he end up all the way over here, in your field?" she asked, tapping the map where they were sitting.

"We figure he walked or ran in," Sheriff Ramsgate spoke up, his tone quiet and gruff. "Got a trail heading out from where the body was found, in the opposite direction. Looks like he was coming over here from his property on foot, and then something either lured him closer or he was running from it and it caught him."

"Someone," Laura corrected him, gently. It was always worth remembering that a killer was just a human. No special powers—at least, she'd never encountered one yet. No superhuman abilities. Just a normal person. They could be defeated by a bullet, or outrun, or outfought, or stopped in other ways. "Any thoughts on who might want to harm Mr. Bluton?"

Ike shook his head. "Jamie was a good kid," he said firmly. "Never heard of anyone having a dispute. We certainly had no problems with him, and we're right next door. Sometimes you do get clashes. Not with him."

Laura nodded, taking this in. "Alright. When you found the body, what do you remember about what you saw, heard, smelled? Anything can help, even if it seems small or insignificant to you."

Ike made a pained face. "I don't recall much," he said. "Sorry. It was a shock, seeing him there. Thought it was kids doing crop circles at first, only to come across him lying there on the ground. I went to grab him—thought he was hurt or maybe sleeping or something, I didn't know why. But I saw the blood on the corn first, splattered across it.

31

Picked him up by the shoulder and I seen his throat. Cut side to side. One of the most gruesome things I ever saw."

Laura watched his face, his body language. His every movement was protective, curling inwards, his shoulders slumping. He was upset. Genuinely so. And, she thought, still more than a little bit shaken.

"Alright," she said. "If you think of anything else later, no matter how small, you give Sheriff Ramsgate a call and let him know. Got that?"

Ike nodded miserably.

"You've done well," she said, injecting her tone with reassuring warmth.

"That was all very helpful," Agent Moore chirped up suddenly, as if she'd finally found ground she knew how to stand on. Laura shot her a quick look, which she apparently ignored. "It must have been a terrible shock for you."

Ike only nodded, though he responded with surprising positivity toward Agent Moore. For Laura, he barely spared another glance.

Laura fought the urge to roll her eyes and got up, nodding a thanks to Pat through the kitchen window beside them. "Sheriff. Back to your station, I should think?"

The Sheriff nodded, getting up. "I'll get the boys to come out here and see about that cordon you wanted."

Laura smiled. At least someone was listening properly. "I take it your county morgue is attached to the station?"

"That it is," Ramsgate replied, starting to walk over to his vehicle. "I'll lead the way. I'm sure you've got a lot you want to see."

32

CHAPTER SEVEN

Laura got out of the car in front of the sheriff's station and county morgue, a squat little one-two of buildings that seemed to have been dumped down in the same parking lot together without much more thought than that. They were an ugly shade of gray, which they had in common with a large majority of the law enforcement buildings Laura had visited around the country. It wasn't as though she expected to feel cheerful when going to look at a body, but something about those buildings always made her feel even worse.

"Bodies first," Laura said, nodding in the direction of the morgue as she pulled up beside the Sheriff—she had enough experience in the field to identify which building was which without having to ask. "Then we'll see about talking to victims' families."

"Oh," Agent Moore said. "Do we have to go look at the bodies? We've already seen the pictures."

Laura blinked at the rookie. "You think the pictures are enough?"

Agent Moore winced. "Aren't they?" she asked.

Her tone was innocent enough that Laura couldn't tell whether she was being serious, or just trying to get out of having to see dead people.

Either way, it didn't matter. The rookie wanted to learn—and she was going to learn. There was no better way to understand the actions of a murderer than to see their direct result—blood, guts, and all. Reading about a killer in a classroom was one thing. Coming up against one was entirely another.

"We need to see for ourselves," Laura said, keeping the explanation short. In her experience, when you went into the details, you just gave people more points to argue against. Besides, it wasn't a debate. This was the job.

She crossed the short walk to the entrance of the morgue, giving the Sheriff a light wave as he headed toward the other building, letting him know via her hands that she was going to look at the body first and would join him again later. He nodded curtly, which sat just fine with her. She wasn't expected to become best friends with him. So long as he complied with what they needed, he could be as grumpy as he liked.

Agent Moore trailed after her like a kid who had been ordered home from school for punishment. She was all but kicking the loose rocks along the edges of the sidewalk. Laura tightened her mouth but said nothing. She wasn't about to get into an argument with a rookie over her attitude. They needed to get in, solve this case, and leave. The less time Laura had to spend with Agent Moore, the better.

She was still hoping, in some small part of herself, that her next case would see her back with her real partner. With Nate. No more rookies.

No point in getting attached.

Laura touched a buzzer on the outside of the door and held up her badge in front of a camera facing downward, and there was a distinct clunking noise as the lock disengaged. The cool interior of the morgue hit her almost as soon as they walked in, even colder than the temperature outside. So did the smell: antibacterial cleaning products, for the most part, but even they could never truly, fully mask the scent of death.

An older man who still seemed quite sprightly in spite of his white hair half-jogged out of a nearby doorway, intercepting them as they hesitated in the main entranceway. There was a reception desk, but it was empty. Laura could hear nothing in the space except for the hum of equipment and, presumably, the air conditioning system. It was eerie, to say the least.

"Ah, welcome!" the medical examiner—so the badge affixed to the front of his white coat identified him—said. "Sheriff Ramsgate did warn me to expect you. I think you're here to look at our two murder victims?"

"That's right." Laura nodded. "Special Agents Frost and Moore. You've got both of them here, correct?"

"That I do," the medical examiner said, turning to lead them back down the hall he'd come from. If Laura wasn't mistaken, he was almost skipping with glee. "Two very unique cases around here. We don't get to see this kind of thing often at all."

"That must be exciting for you," Laura said dryly.

"Oh, absolutely!" the medical examiner exclaimed. "I mean, of course, it's terribly tragic, you understand—but I'm thrilled to be able to use some of those rusty skills I haven't been able to really get into since I was last in a city. It's been—goodness, now I think about it, probably thirty years."

"It's been thirty years since you worked on a dead body?" Agent Moore piped up, clearly absolutely astonished. Laura shot her a look. The rookie's auburn hair was practically bouncing along behind her in that ponytail.

The medical examiner laughed heartily. "No, no, we get our share of death here. As does anyone else," he said. "No, it's usually just heart attacks and the like. It's been thirty years since I worked on a brutal, bloody murder like this. Even the last time we *did* have a murder, that was poison."

"You find this exciting?" Moore asked, again with wide eyes, but this time also a note of horror in her voice.

The medical examiner glanced back with a slightly guilty look and cleared his throat. "Well, I mean, you know. Terrible for the families. Absolute tragedy, of course."

"Don't worry," Laura said, with a grim smile. "I know what you mean. The 'death' part of it kind of loses its impact after a while, doesn't it?"

"It does," the medical examiner replied, with a relieved tone, as he led them to a table which Laura could have probably drawn with her eyes closed. It was the same as all the others. Metal slab on wheels, white sheet, clearly a body underneath it. "Apart from the kids. The kids are the worst."

"Agreed," Laura said. "Right, let's have a look at Mr. Bluton, shall we?"

"Certainly," the medical examiner said, and whipped up the edge of the white sheet, unveiling the naked corpse of a man. He was slashed not just across the throat, but also multiple times over his torso. To Laura's amateur eye, it looked like most of them would easily have been enough to kill him, even if the neck hadn't been cut.

There was a retching noise, and Laura and the medical examiner both swung around as one to see Agent Moore bending over a trash can beside a desk.

"Are you alright?" Laura asked. She was trying to be charitable— rookies did often find themselves unwell when they first saw a body. And this one was particularly gruesome. It was also true that Agent Moore had only made a fool of herself in front of the medical examiner, not the Sheriff.

But still. If you wanted everyone on the case to know you were a rookie, this was one surefire way to do it.

"I'm okay," Agent Moore said, turning around with an unconvincing smile. She put the trash can back down on the ground. "I held it in. Mostly." She still looked green. Laura took a practiced step away from her just in case, then turned her attention back to the body.

"This was vicious," Laura said, thinking out loud. "Personal, it looks like. You don't harm someone this badly unless you really want them to suffer—and you want to make absolutely sure they're dead. The number of wounds even goes beyond that. The cuts were made by a blade of some kind?"

"Mm," the medical examiner said, tilting his head to one side. "Of some kind. I'd definitely say a blade, but this isn't an ordinary knife. It's hard to tell if there is any mark on the blade, or to get an idea of the shape of it, because the cuts are done in such a way—it's a real slash from one side to the other, quick as you like, no hesitation. What I can tell you is that it's very, very sharp—the skin seems to part like butter. As for the size, I would say it's very long."

"Nothing else of forensic interest on the body?" Laura asked. She reached for the white sheet as if she was being helpful. The truth was, she wanted a chance to touch the skin of the corpse, to see if it would trigger something for her.

"Nothing, I'm afraid," the medical examiner said. Laura pulled the sheet over, just lightly brushing her little finger against the arm, tensing when a new headache hit her—

She was looking out over a field. Maybe the one she'd been to earlier, maybe not. It was impossible to tell. No markers on the skyline, no visible landmarks—just corn, swaying around her in the breeze under a bright sky.

There were several men standing around, talking, hands shoved in their pockets. They were standing on a dirt road; if this was the Brown farm, then Laura was confused, because the track was much thinner and less defined than she remembered.

The men were having some kind of conversation—Laura couldn't follow it. Something about the corn. They talked lazily, hands shoved in the pockets of worn and patched coveralls. One of them was wearing an old-fashioned kind of hat and smoking on a pipe. He looked like a transplant from a different century.

No—they all did. Laura looked at the other two men, taking them in as much as she could. Their clothes seemed like they weren't what she would expect—even from a rural community. It was hard to put a finger on why, exactly—something about with the style, even though they were perfectly workable garments, just felt off. And there were other hints... a pocket watch in one pocket, nothing on their wrists. No sign of a cell phone, even though it might have been in a pocket; Laura just couldn't see any of these men knowing what to do with one. Their shoes were old-fashioned, too, clunky and battered. Not like the shoes Ike Brown had been wearing—modern waterproof boots.

This was all wrong.

36

All three of them turned suddenly to look at something behind Laura, as if they had heard a sound—

And Laura was back in the morgue, looking down at a body neatly covered with a sheet.

What in the hell had she just seen?

"This is poor Miss Michaels," the medical examiner was saying, turning Laura's and Agent Moore's attention to the next trolley. She shot a glance at the rookie, her head only throbbing a little as she did so. The other agent looked even more pale at the idea of seeing another body.

Only a mild headache, and it was fading already. That was odd. Usually, Laura knew that the intensity of the headache was linked to the urgency of the vision. The more pain she was left with, the more imminent the scene. But this time, it was almost as if the vision she'd had was of something that would happen in twenty years.

Or a hundred years ago.

Was that what she had seen? The past?

The medical examiner was embarking on a passionate and detailed description of the wounds the first victim to be found, Janae Michaels, had suffered. Laura let her mind drift off just a short distance, keeping aware enough that she would notice if he pointed out anything unusual or different from what they had already seen on the other body.

It would make sense if her vision was from a time gone by. The road that wasn't quite as wide yet. The clothing the farmers were wearing, and the lack of any sign of technology—she hadn't been able to hear or see cars, phones, planes overhead, anything that might signal they were in modern times.

But if that was the case, then it also didn't make sense at all, because Laura had visions of things that were yet to happen *in the future.*

She'd had visions of the past once before. If this was another, it meant that her dubious gift was getting more and more out of control. The rules were changing on her, and she hated it. It made her feel dizzy, unmoored, helpless. Like she was at the mercy of it, not the other way around.

She'd always been at its mercy. That was the problem with not really knowing how her visions worked. She couldn't control them. Couldn't start or stop them.

Sometimes, she couldn't even understand them.

She had no idea what this vision could even mean, except that she was starting to think that maybe this whole case had something to do with the farm itself, or with the field even...

"What do you think, Agent Frost?" Agent Moore blurted out, making Laura look at her.

Laura blinked. She hadn't been listening at all. "What do *you* think?" she asked, trying to pretend she was turning this into a learning moment.

"We should probably talk to the families like you said, right?" Agent Moore said. "Get some more perspective?"

"Exactly," Laura said grandly, as if she was impressed with Agent Moore for getting the right answer. "Come on. Let's go next door and see if the Sheriff can point us in the right direction."

CHAPTER EIGHT

Laura strode into the Sheriff's office after a brief knock on the door; she'd seen through the glass that he wasn't alone, but that was the point. The middle-aged woman who worked on the desk at the front door had already informed her that Mrs. Bluton had just arrived from her trip out of town.

"Ah, Agent Frost," Sheriff Ramsgate said. He had a slight look of relief about him. He cast an eye toward Mrs. Bluton before looking back at her, and Laura noticed that the woman was actively crying into a tissue. "Maria, these are the FBI agents I was telling you about. They're in charge of the case now, and they're going to make sure your Jamie gets the justice he deserves."

Laura sucked in a breath. She wished people wouldn't make promises like that—and especially not on her behalf. She'd do her best, but nothing was ever guaranteed.

"Mrs. Bluton, we're very sorry for your loss," Laura said. "I wonder if now is a good time to talk to you a little about your husband, see if we can't get to the bottom of this?"

She sat down in one of the chairs at the Sheriff's desk, turning and angling it toward Mrs. Bluton first, having no intention of taking no for an answer. Agent Moore hovered in the doorway for a moment, seeing that there was nowhere else to sit. Laura caught her eye and then shot a glance toward a low filing cabinet at the side of the room. Agent Moore took the hint with a grateful expression and perched on the edge of it, holding her hands together in her lap as though she was waiting for the grown-ups to talk.

"Yes, I suppose I can." Maria Bluton sniffed, raising her head from the tissue. She was wearing mascara which had streaked in ugly black lines down her face, giving her a look as though she had been saved from drowning. Together with her travel-rumpled clothes and messy hairstyle—thrown back into a bun as if she had paid little thought to it—she painted a clear picture of a woman in the throes of grief.

Not that that necessarily meant she had nothing to do with her husband's death. Laura knew enough to be cautious in these circumstances.

"I'm sorry to have to ask this, but was there anyone you can think of who might have wanted to harm your husband for any reason?" she asked, for a kick-off.

"No!" Maria burst out, shaking her head wildly. "No, Jamie got along with everyone. Everyone we knew, which wasn't a whole lot of people. We've had to keep our heads down. There's been so much to do at the farm over the past few years. He knew some people here from when he was younger, but a lot of the kids he went to school with have grown up and moved away. I don't know why anyone would have any reason to hurt him—to want him d—" She cut herself off on the last word, a choking sob filling her mouth instead.

"Alright," Laura said with feeling, trying to reassure the woman as best as she could. "That's great. You're doing great. Did you talk with your husband at all while you were away?"

"Of course," Maria said. "We were texting all the time, and I called him every night."

"Did he at all seem different to you? Was he worried about anything or did he notice anything suspicious?"

"No," Maria said, wiping her eyes only to smear the mascara more badly across her face. "Everything was fine. I don't know why someone would do this. We didn't even have anything worth stealing, except the equipment!"

Laura glanced up at the Sheriff. "Was anything taken?"

"We don't believe anyone entered the farmhouse," he said. "We'll have to ask you to take a look at the machinery, Maria, but it looked to us as though everything was where it should be."

"I just don't understand," Maria went on. "Jamie never hurt anyone. Why would someone want him gone? Why would they want to leave my kids without a father?"

The mention of children made Laura wince. They hadn't gone into the details of the family enough, but she did remember Ike saying earlier that James Bluton was a family man. Laura figured that Mrs. Bluton must have left the children with her family, rather than bringing them to the scene of their father's death.

"How old are your children?" Laura asked.

"One is five years old, the other is six," Maria said. "We were visiting my family and their father's."

"Their father's?" Laura asked, picking up on the strange phrasing. Not *Jamie's* or *my husband's*.

"The children are mine, not Jamie's," Maria said. "I got into a relationship with a... a bad man. I got out of it and Jamie, he kind of rescued me when I was on my own. Took on the kids and looked after them like they were his blood. He was... he was everything we needed." Her eyes were misty again, fresh fat tears sliding down her face when she blinked her lashes.

"Where is the children's father?" Laura asked, seeing the suspect immediately. "Did he know you were living here with Jamie?"

Maria shook her head. "He died two years ago," she said. "Bar fight. Now I'm all those kids have."

"That must suck, having to raise them as a single mom," Agent Moore spoke up unexpectedly. Looking at her, Laura saw she was shaking her head in sympathy. "I'm *so* sorry."

There was a pause in the room, a beat. No one spoke. Maria was looking at Agent Moore with a kind of horror for a moment, and the Sheriff even looked somewhat angry. Laura cleared her throat. She needed to get the interview back on track, rather than letting it be derailed by the interruption. The whole flow was off now, but she could get it back.

"Did you take part in any local parent groups or community meetups?" Laura asked, deciding to proceed as though Agent Moore hadn't even said anything.

"No, not really," Maria said, sniffling. "I didn't have time to go with the boys. And there wasn't much of it going on around here, anyway. Everyone already knows each other, so why have set times and places to meet up? It's been a bit isolating, to be honest."

She suddenly burst into a fresh peal of tears. Laura could easily imagine why. Agent Moore had just reminded her that she was going to have to do it all on her own now. The farm, the children, everything. More likely, she would have to sell. There was no way a single woman with small children could manage that all on her own, and it sounded as though there was no one else left on James's side. She'd verify that later with the Sheriff, just in case she felt she needed to talk to anyone else.

"And James, was he part of any groups? Perhaps a farming community?"

Maria shook her head again. "There are events all year long, but in the past couple of years we never really managed to get to them. After we moved here, we were too busy. Then things died down a little but it was harvest season and Jamie needed every spare moment I had. After that I got pregnant again and I couldn't drink—which is the main point of all those events anyway. I, um. I had a miscarriage last year." A shadow passed over her face—most likely the realization that there would never be another baby now.

Laura nodded sympathetically, but inside, she didn't like what she was hearing. All of this was adding up to the victim having no reason to fear violence from any sector. If there was no one who was angry with him, then there was no one who had the motive to attack him so viciously and deliberately end his life. She was beginning to think that maybe the victim had been hiding something, even from his wife. If this was a personally directed attack, it was the only thing that made sense.

They needed to connect the two victims, find out what they had in common and why it would have made them a target.

"Do you or your husband know Janae Michaels?" Laura asked, naming the second victim. "Even if you've only seen each other around town, anything like that?"

"No," Maria said, shaking her head slowly. She looked at the Sheriff questioningly, then back at Laura. "Who is that?" She had stopped, a break in her tears, no doubt because she was now wondering who this woman was who seemed in some way to be connected to her husband's death.

"Are you aware of any link, Sheriff?" Laura asked, instead of answering the grieving widow's question.

"I'm not," Sheriff Ramsgate said, his tone reserved. It was clear that he didn't want to give away any details of the case that he had not yet been cleared to.

"Alright," Laura said, standing up. "We'll leave you there, Mrs. Bluton. Thank you so much for everything you've told us. If you do think of something suspicious, or you come across something that you think might be related to what happened, don't hesitate to get back in touch with us or the Sheriff."

"You can call me anytime," Agent Moore said, jumping forward with a business card outstretched in her hand. She practically dove in front of Laura to make sure that she offered it to the woman, and Laura let her. It was always tedious, having to field calls from grieving family members when they really had nothing extra to add. Laura suspected that this was going to be the case with Mrs. Bluton, and that the only calls they might really expect would be chasing up and asking if they had solved the case yet. Agent Moore could deal with those if she was so eager to.

That done, Laura nodded at the Sheriff and again at Mrs. Bluton. "We really are sorry for your loss," she said, as a parting comment, before leading Agent Moore out of the room.

She didn't know where she was heading, and she couldn't exactly ask the Sheriff. She didn't want to stop him from giving his condolences to the woman, who was after all part of the local community that he served. They would just find somewhere and pitch up, and if they had to move later, so be it.

Using her knowledge of Sheriff's stations and precincts from across the country, Laura moved down the hall in what she suspected might be the right direction. Sure enough, after the Sheriff's office she found a door leading into a more open area, a kind of bullpen, if very small. There were only three desks, one of which was occupied for the time being. The deputy there was a rail-thin man who looked even older than the Sheriff was, his hands typing slowly away at a computer that might well have been older than Laura herself.

"Are these desks in use?" Laura asked, pointing to the two workstations that seemed unoccupied.

The old deputy looked up. "Not at the moment," he said.

That was good enough. Laura was fairly sure that he was being overly sarcastic—since the lack of people sitting at them made it very obvious that they were not in use *at the moment*—but it was a good excuse for later if they did turn out to be sitting in an inconvenient spot. She chose a desk at random, gesturing toward the seat next to it that would no doubt normally be reserved for criminals and taking the desk chair for herself.

Once Agent Moore was seated, Laura pulled out the file she'd brought with her—the briefing notes, folded in two in order to fit in the inner pocket of her jacket. She smoothed them out and leafed through the pages. "We need to do a bit of research and see if we can connect these two," she said. "There must be something they have in common. Hopefully, something easy to spot."

"How can we check that?" Agent Moore asked.

Laura experimentally moved the mouse attached to the computer they were sitting at. The screen activated onto the desktop, which she was fairly sure constituted some kind of regulatory breach if not the law. It shouldn't have been possible for just anyone to access it. Still, not waiting for IT support was convenient in this case.

"You start with these," Laura said, tapping the briefing documents against the table and then handing them over. "They have the basic stats pulled from county records—name, age, place and date of birth, height, and so on. Just look for anything that matches. I'm going to do a little bit of search engine magic and see if I can't dig anything up."

It was an easy enough process. She started by searching "James Bluton" and "Janae Michaels" together, then changing the name to Jamie just in case. Nothing came up at all. Searching the names separately brought up social media pages and a couple of mentions in local papers—one for a farming-related story and one for a school sports team from about ten years ago.

Nothing related at all.

"I can't see anything that matches up," Agent Moore said, putting the files aside with a sigh.

"Nothing here either," Laura confirmed. "What did you find out about Janae Michaels?"

"Just that she was twenty-five years old, she was also a local but lived in town rather than out on a farm, and she worked from home for a tech startup on their customer support line." Agent Moore shrugged, rubbing at one of her eyes. "There's not much else to tell. She was attacked in her own backyard, but it only had a low fence that would have been easy to climb over. No DNA evidence recovered at the scene."

Laura nodded. She knew as much from reading the briefing documents previously, but it was aways good to have a refresher. "Then there's no link between them," she said, swiveling her chair thoughtfully. Of course, she knew that wasn't the end of the story. It couldn't be. They had missed something.

There had to be some kind of link.

They just had to figure out how to find it.

"Right," Laura said decisively. "If there's nothing that comes up at surface level, then we just have to look deeper."

"How are we going to do that?" Agent Moore asked.

Laura cracked her knuckles. "Get your phone," she said. "We've got some calls to make."

CHAPTER NINE

The basement where he sat was cold, quiet, and still. The perfect environment for cleaning up and preparing for the next one.

No one would disturb him down here. Why would they? And even if they did, he would hear their steps on the stairs, hear the door above opening, and have plenty of time to put away what he was working on.

He dipped the rag into the laundry room sink again, taking in more of the pink-stained water and then rubbing it carefully over the next part of the sickle blade. Each single speck of blood had to be cleansed and removed, leaving the sickle as spotless and shining as it had been when he first got it. It was slow work, but he didn't mind. It was worth it, to keep the blade as strong and righteous as it needed to be.

That's right, she said, in that way she had. The way that wasn't out loud. It was inside the chambers of his head, echoing, telling him all he needed to know in the clearest of terms. *Make sure you get all of it.*

"What's next on the agenda?" he asked, dipping the cloth again. He eyed the rest of his setup. The polishing cloth and whetting stone were ready for him. She would know he didn't mean which step was next in cleaning and polishing the scythe. It was a broader question that he asked. She'd never had any trouble understanding what he meant when he spoke to her. It was like she could hear his thoughts as well as sending him her own.

You've done so well already, she said. *But there must be more. We have only just begun.*

"I know that," he replied. "I'm ready. Don't worry. I won't let you down. No matter how many of them it takes, I'm willing to get it done."

Are you ready to take another as soon as tomorrow? Even tonight?

"Of course." He put down the cleaning rag for a moment, intending to show just how serious he was. "Whatever you need me to do, whoever you think should be next. I'll follow your lead. Even if I have to take out a kid, I'll do it. I promise."

That won't be necessary.

"Not ever?"

Not yet.

He thought about that, turning it over in his mind.

"Well," he said, at last, reaching for the cleaning rag again, "I'm ready. I mean it. I'm as committed to this as you are."

He felt her amusement, even though she didn't say anything at first. It was like a warmth spreading over him. She didn't think he could possibly be committed to the same level as she was, but she appreciated him saying it all the same.

There's another one you should focus on next, she said. *I'll guide you to them. You must end them. End the line. Finish this. There's still such a long way to go. We can't afford to get distracted now.*

"I know," he said, cleaning the last drop of blood completely off the blade. He took the cleaning rag and dumped it into an empty metal bin, where he could burn it later when it had dried off. Once that was gone, along with the polishing cloth, there would only be the blade itself to incriminate him.

Not that he really minded if people knew he'd done it. He was philosophical about that. As far as he was concerned, he was a hero. Doing what needed to be done. They would probably write songs about him.

He just needed to keep getting away with it until he'd finished the job—or there wouldn't be anything to sing about at all.

"Tell me where to go next," he said, picking up the scythe and laying the blade against the whetstone, ready to get it sharp enough to kill.

CHAPTER TEN

"I'm just not seeing it," Laura sighed, rubbing her hands over her face. It was only mid-morning on their first day of the case, but she was already feeling frustrated.

The first thing you needed in a case with multiple victims was the link. The thing that connected them. Maybe they were all acting coaches who trained the same actor. Maybe they were all twins. Maybe they'd all had a near-death experience which should have claimed their life, but didn't. Whatever it was—there was always something.

The fact she hadn't found something yet didn't mean it wasn't there. It just meant she wasn't doing her job very successfully.

There was one thing she knew for sure. There *had* to be a link between the two victims. If this was some kind of random spree killer, then it might be hard to trace. It might even just be that they had both interacted with the killer at some point. But if they had, that was something they might be able to trace, too, with a lot of work.

Whatever it was, it was beyond the obvious. Under the surface. Something that wasn't public knowledge. And if it was something that not many people knew about, then the killer would be someone from a small pool of people. If they could figure this out, they could find him.

They needed to figure it out.

"Well, I mean," Agent Moore said, shrugging carefully, "she was single, right?"

"Yes," Laura said. She frowned. "You think that's relevant? It's not a match. He was married."

"Yes, but his wife was out of town," Agent Moore said. She sucked in a breath and shook her head, as if what she was about to say was terrible. "I don't like to think the worst of people. But do you think it was possible they were... you know?"

Laura stared at her for a moment. Agent Moore made a face, a kind of strained expression with her pink-lipsticked mouth.

"Having an affair?" Laura suggested, when the end of the sentence was not forthcoming.

"Yeah," Agent Moore said, hushed, as if she didn't want the old deputy to overhear such a scandalous thought.

Laura thought about it, then shook her head. "We would have seen something. We have all of their social media accounts, we've accessed their private messages and their emails. There's nothing even remotely suggestive from anyone, and no contact between the two of them."

"That we know of," Agent Moore insisted. "What if they used secret, private accounts and made sure to log out of them every time? Or, what if they sent each other messages and then deleted them as soon as they'd finished the conversation, so no one could find them by accident?"

Laura gave Agent Moore a sideways look. "You sound like you know a lot about how to hide talking to someone."

"What?" Agent Moore's cheeks blazed bright red. "No! Only because I saw it on a detective show on TV!"

Laura chuckled to herself and shook her head. The rookie was green in more ways than one. Easy to tease. "Well, if they did that, we'll have to find evidence elsewhere. Then we can ask the tech forensics team to dig into their browser history, IP addresses, their devices, and whatever else they need to try and figure it out. But we can't really ask them to undertake that big of a search without having something to base it on, and right now that's nothing more than a guess."

"So, what do we do?"

What did they do? Laura thought the question over, searching her mind like it was a database of past cases, looking for the next direction to go in.

The most useful thing, of course, would be to have a vision. But while she was sitting there waiting for it, it wasn't going to happen. The visions didn't just happen on their own. She had to touch something, to come into contact with it. Something linked with the vision she would have. It could be anything, even something that had the barest possible link. Something the killer had touched.

Unfortunately, with the lack of physical evidence involved in the case so far, they had nothing like that sitting around the Sheriff's station. Nothing was going to come to her if she just sat here and did nothing and waited. Besides, she also needed to do real investigation work—not just to try to catch the killer faster, but because that would also help to give her excuses she could use to explain away how she knew what the visions told her.

Laura drummed her hands on the desk. "We need another lead," she said. "Let's look in another direction. The data from the telephone companies that we asked for should be coming through soon, and we'll be able to read it and find out if they ever called or texted each other. What about the bank statements? Have they been sent over yet?"

Agent Moore hummed, tapping on her cell phone to open up her emails. "Yes! Looks like they came in about five minutes ago."

"Great, then let's get started," Laura said. "Forward the records from Janae Michaels to me. You look through James Bluton's. Anything suspicious, you flag it up. Anything like a bar or restaurant, you flag it up. When we compare, we might get something."

Agent Moore nodded, biting her short fingernail with concentration as she sent the data over. "Done," she said. "I'll start reading it now."

They lapsed into silence for a while, each of them barking out the occasional restaurant chain brand. Once, James had taken out $300 from an ATM with no explanation, but there was no repeat of the incident.

"We can ask his wife about that later," Laura said. "Listen to this— last month, Janae Michaels stayed in a hotel for two nights. But it was only about two hours out of town. That's not far, right? You'd almost prefer to just drive there and back again rather than having to pay for a hotel, don't you think?"

Agent Moore pursed her lips. "Maybe. I only learned to drive last year, so before that I would have taken a train or bus and then stayed in a hotel to avoid the hassle."

Laura blinked at her. "Why didn't you know how to drive?"

"Because of the commune," Agent Moore said cheerfully. "We didn't do driving lessons. But I needed a license to get into the FBI, so I learned."

Laura shook her head in wonder. "Alright, so there could be a reason for staying at a hotel two hours ago that was innocent," she said. "What about him? Bluton? Where was he around those dates? If we can place him in the same town, then maybe we can say they did know each other after all."

"Hang on," Agent Moore said, her voice rising higher and getting faster. "What did you say the hotel was called?"

"I didn't," Laura said. "The Great Maple Ohio."

"This is it!" Agent Moore exclaimed, pushing her cell across the table and tapping the screen excitedly. "Look! Two nights' stay. He was there on the exact same dates!"

Laura examined the line items carefully, making sure the rest of the entries were different. She wasn't about to accuse the rookie of being stupid, but things happened sometimes. It would have been

49

embarrassing if it turned out they were both looking at the records of the same person.

But they weren't. Michaels and Bluton had spent their money on different things while they were out in that other town.

This was a lead.

"Well, well, well," Laura said, looking the items over again. She hit search on the computer, looking up the details of the hotel. They could call, but if they were going to do this properly, they should go there; a two-hour drive wasn't much. The hotel might give them another lead, and there was the possibility of watching the CCTV footage or showing the photographs of the deceased to different staff members. This would be a much easier and more comprehensive investigation if they went there in person.

And, against all odds, it looked as though the rookie might have good instincts after all. There was actually a real possibility that she might have been right about there being an affair.

"Grab your coat," Laura said, nodding to the back of Agent Moore's chair. "I'll go tell the Sheriff we're heading out for a while."

CHAPTER ELEVEN

Laura stretched her hands over her head for a moment as she waited outside the hotel for Agent Moore to catch up. Laura was stiff after a night of air travel and then a two-hour drive, but she was apparently still more sprightly than the rookie. Agent Moore had fallen asleep in the passenger seat on the way, and was only just managing to walk a little unsteadily up the path from the parking lot where Laura had left her as she jumped out of the car.

"Come on," she said impatiently. "It took us long enough to get here without adding more delays."

"Right, right," Agent Moore said, stifling a yawn. "Sorry! I'm not used to traveling at night."

"You'll get over that," Laura said, half joking—but half serious. They traveled a lot for cases, and without fail, Laura could almost always guarantee they would be stuck on a red-eye. The Bureau had a budget, after all.

"This is the place, then," Agent Moore said, glancing up at the façade of the hotel as Laura started to step inside.

"No, I thought I'd stop somewhere random along the way," Laura said. Then she stopped herself, taking a deep breath. She was being unnecessarily snippy. She didn't like the fact that the rookie had managed to fit in a nap—she was jealous, truth be told—and she was still on edge about... well, everything. Nate. The changes in her visions. The headache that never truly went away anymore, just stayed throbbing at the back of her skull—begging her to douse it with a drink that she couldn't let herself have. "Yes, this is it. We'll talk to the reception staff, see if they recognize anything about the bookings first." Her tone was softer for the second part, trying to defuse the meanness of the first.

"Sorry," Agent Moore mumbled quietly, and Laura felt a stab of regret. She needed to remember that she was basically working with a kid right out of training. Annoying as that was, it was Rondelle's fault she was stuck with Moore, not the rookie's.

Laura led the way to the front desk, taking out her badge and holding it up until she was acknowledged. "Hi, we're working on an open investigation right now," she said. "Special Agents Frost and Moore. I need to take a look at your guest records."

"Um," the young woman behind the desk said.

"We're with the FBI," Laura said, waiting for this to sink in. The receptionist was obviously inexperienced and had no idea what she was supposed to do in this kind of situation. When she still hesitated, Laura added: "We're investigating a murder."

"Let me get my manager," the woman suggested.

"Great idea," Laura said, leaning her hand on the counter to tap her fingernails restlessly as the young woman disappeared.

"Do people not just usually look scared and give us what we need?" Agent Moore asked in a stage whisper. "That's what they do on TV."

"Sadly, people in the real world are both more suspicious and more knowledgeable of their rights," Laura said. "If she comes back with a manager who doesn't want to help, we could be stuck trying to chase down a warrant for the rest of the day."

"Oh," Agent Moore said, in a tone which implied she very much hoped that didn't turn out to be the case.

When the manager did appear a moment later, however, Laura breathed an internal sigh of relief. Outwardly, she remained stoic, straightening her back just a little more to give her that air of steely authority. The manager was a middle-aged man with a receding hairline, a nervous chin, and a duck of his head that indicated he was scared of talking to them before they had even begun.

"Um, good morning, ladies," he said. "I mean, Agents? Joanna told me you're FBI agents."

"That's right," Laura confirmed, showing her badge again. "We need to check out your guest records for last month. I have a couple of credit charges for rooms here and I need to verify that the people in question were actually guests here, rather than simply paying for someone else's stay."

"Alright," he said, nodding slowly and then beginning to type rapidly into a computer behind the desk. "That doesn't seem like an unreasonable request. What were the dates in question?"

Laura gave them, then the names of the two victims. The manager nodded all the while, as if trying desperately to show that he was cooperating and understood everything she was saying.

"Okay. The names in our database match up," he said, looking up expectantly. "Those are the guests who were registered here with us on those two nights."

"And do you take ID checks at all?" Laura asked.

"Yes," he said, then hesitated. "Although, we don't have any record of them, so I can't show it to you."

"The point is I need to be absolutely sure it was those two people who checked in," Laura said. "Were they staying in different rooms?"

"Yes, 203 and... 306."

Different floors. Laura mused on that for a moment. There was still nothing to prove that they weren't there together. If they were being as cautious as possible to stop Bluton's wife from finding out, then they might have paid for separate rooms but snuck in together. "Were you working that day?" she asked.

The manager frowned, clicking onto what Laura assumed was probably the staff roster. "No..." He brightened, glancing over his shoulder. "But Joanna was."

The young receptionist looked nervous to be called forward again. She had her hands clasped in front of her uncertainly, and kept them that way as she stepped back to her normal place behind the desk, replacing the manager. "Did you need me to check anything?"

"Just tell me if you recognize these people," Laura said. She took a moment to open up the right images on her phone—the ones where James Bluton and Janae Michaels were alive, not their crime scene photos.

Joanna looked for a short moment, then nodded enthusiastically. "Mm-hm. Both of them checked in here. I'm sure of it. I think I saw them checking out as well—Rachel was on the front desk that day, though, and I was running room service."

"Then we probably need to talk to Rachel as well," Laura noted. "Did you see them talking to one another?"

Joanna shook her head no. "It was a busy day, but I think they checked in at different times."

"Yes, the system recorded them as checking in several hours apart," the manager confirmed. "Looks like the checkout time was different, too."

"Alright." So, if they were really having an affair, they had taken steps to cover their tracks carefully. But there was one factor that they might still not have accounted for. Well, two. The surveillance footage was one. "Can I look at your camera footage?"

The manager winced. "This was just over a month ago, so I'm afraid it will have been overwritten by now."

Laura resisted the urge to facepalm. That left just one avenue. "Do you know who cleaned the rooms on those days?" Laura asked.

The manager checked his list again. "Oh, yes. That was the same cleaner on both days. Luisa Lopez."

"Great. Then can we speak to Luisa?"

"Um," the manager said, and Laura's spine tingled. "The thing is, we haven't seen Luisa in a few days. She was supposed to come in for her shift, but she never did."

Every red flag in Laura's head went up, alarm bells screaming. That was incredibly suspicious behavior, and the timing fit perfectly. "Is that normal for her, to take off for a while?"

"Not at all," the manager said, shaking his head. "If we had that kind of behavior on a regular basis, she would be fired. To be honest, if she does show up now, she'll have a hard time keeping her job as it is. She had an exemplary record before now, but there are very few good reasons for not showing up without calling ahead to let us know. Being in the hospital is the only one I can think of."

"Or being dead," Agent Moore said, making a face that suggested the manager should have thought before he spoke.

"If she was dead," he said, clearly not getting the same vibe of authority from her that he got from Laura, "we wouldn't be giving her any more shifts either."

"Alright," Laura said, cutting them off before the conversation could descend into an argument or a battle of wits. "Do you have Luisa's home address on record? I'd like to go and speak with her if I can track her down."

The manager hesitated only for a second—probably wondering whether he was supposed to protect the privacy of his employees—before clicking something on the screen. Nearby, a printer whirred to life. Perhaps his protective instinct didn't extend to those who had failed to show up for work for two days in a row.

Laura took the printout from his outstretched hand. "Any other records or data you have, make sure they aren't deleted or overwritten," she said. "It might be important to keep the surveillance footage, too. See if you can get onto the security company or someone who controls how often they reuse the tapes, so you can put a halt on it. We may need more dates looking into later."

He nodded smartly. "Yes, ma'am."

Laura turned, handing the paper to Agent Moore. "Let's get that entered into the GPS," she said.

"What do you think?" Agent Moore asked, as they stepped outside and away from listening ears. "She's a suspect, right? This maid?"

"Yes, maybe no," Laura said. "There are other possibilities. Maybe she saw something she wasn't meant to see and the killer has gone after her as well. Maybe she was involved in the cover-up. Maybe she was threatened by the victims and decided to get them first—or maybe someone paid her off and she doesn't need the job anymore."

"Well, which is it?" Agent Moore asked with a frown as she got into the passenger side of the car.

Laura joined her in the driver's seat. "There's only one way to find out," she said, switching on the ignition.

CHAPTER TWELVE

Laura checked the GPS against the apartment block in front of them. It rose into the sky, a concrete tower that blocked out the pale winter sun. It was inhospitable-looking, to say the least. Someone had attempted to grow some flowers in a box outside the ground-floor windows, but they were all shriveled and dead.

"This is it," Laura confirmed. "What was the number again?"

"One hundred twenty-three," Agent Moore replied, scanning the printout that the hotel manager had given them.

Laura nodded. "At least it's on the first floor." She killed the engine and climbed out of the car, eager to get started. It could be that they would get this all wrapped up within the next half an hour and be on their way home before the end of the day, but she had her doubts. For one thing, the viciousness of the attacks and the use of the blade seemed to point to a man. But then, strange things did happen. Maybe they would arrest this maid, she would confess everything, and the case would be done.

She could hope, anyway.

There was someone just leaving the apartment block, and Laura rushed forward to grab the door before it closed. It was a huge advantage, not having to ask to be buzzed inside. It meant that their suspect would not have time to escape down the staircase to the emergency exit, or climb out of a window onto the fire escape. It meant she wouldn't have time to hide or destroy any evidence.

Laura led the way to the elevators and punched the button impatiently a few times, the whirring of the mechanism indicating that the metal box was on its slow journey toward them. Better to take the elevator than the stairs. They might need enough energy for a chase if they confronted her and she managed to slip by them.

It finally pinged open and the two agents stepped inside, Laura instinctively turning back to face the way they had come in so that she would be ready to get out. Agent Moore, on the other hand, stayed facing toward her, meaning they were left face to face as the elevator moved them upward.

"This is so exciting," Agent Moore confessed. She had a little bright spark in her eyes to show the truth in her words. "I can kind of see what you meant earlier. About cases being thrilling even though they're tragic. I can't wait to see if it was her that did it. If it was, we can get our first case solved in just a few hours! Won't that be amazing?"

"Your first case," Laura corrected her with a wry look. "Very far from mine. Don't count your chickens just yet."

"I know, I know," Agent Moore said, bouncing on her heels. She was grinning. It was quite disconcerting, being this close up to that much enthusiasm.

The elevator doors slid open, and Laura stepped out into the hall. Just as disconcerting as her refusal to turn around in there was Agent Moore's habit of waiting for Laura to lead, meaning she had to actually step past the rookie to get out. Laura was beginning to get the impression that when she said she had grown up on a commune, she really meant that she'd spent almost her whole life in one. It was like she didn't even understand the simple etiquette of riding an elevator.

Laura pushed her temporary partner's strangeness to the back of her mind and carried on walking down the hall, searching the numbers on the doors they passed. One sixteen—one seventeen—one eighteen. They were heading in the right direction, that was for sure.

Looking up at the end of the hallway, Laura spotted it. Apartment one twenty-three was the one right at the end of the hall, the door facing back inward toward them as they approached. Better for approaching visibility, worse for approaching with stealth. Laura picked up her pace. The last thing they needed was for their suspect to sense they were coming before they even got there.

She stopped right in front of the door and knocked hard, saying nothing. There was a moment's pause in which she almost thought no one was home; then, hushed voices revealed the lie in that impression.

Then there was a kind of shuffling and scraping noise, and Laura put two and two together, a vivid image forming in her mind's eye.

"The window," she snapped at Agent Moore. "She's trying to climb out the window! Get around there, now!"

Agent Moore nodded and shot away, her feet thudding down the hall as she ran, bypassing the elevators and rushing right down the stairs. Laura hammered hard on the door again, stepping closer to hear as much as she could through it. "Stop what you're doing!" she yelled. "FBI!"

The only thing she heard in response was a sudden crash, as though of a slide-up window that had been allowed to drop closed on its own. Downstairs, she heard the buzz of the building's main door being unlocked from the inside—no doubt Agent Moore stepping out into the street. Beyond that, she could hear nothing; the noise from the street was insulated enough by the building that she had no idea what was going on.

Until a woman's voice inside the apartment began shouting. "Stop! Stop! Leave him alone!"

Laura knocked hard on the door again. "Let me in and we can discuss this," she shouted. "We're with the FBI." It was always worth repeating, just in case the message had not sunk in the first time.

There was a rapid collection of footsteps and then the rattle of a chain, and the apartment door opened. Behind it was standing a petite Latina woman, long dark hair up in a bun on the top of her head, dressed in a two-piece running suit in a deep pink velour fabric. "Let him go," she pleaded. "He hasn't done anything. I swear!"

Laura stepped past her into the apartment and headed to the window, which was very clearly the one she had heard sliding up and down. Lifting it, she stuck her head outside, looking down at where Agent Moore appeared to have tackled a man to the ground.

"Cuff him and bring him back up here," she shouted. Then she paused, watching. "Can you do that, or do you need help?"

"I've got it!" Agent Moore shouted out gamely. Her tongue stuck out of the side of her mouth as she grabbed the cuffs from her belt and started putting them on the man's wrists. At least he couldn't see her face, pinned to the ground as he was. Laura shook her head and leaned back inside, turning to look at the petite woman who had answered the door.

"So," Laura said. "You're Luisa Lopez, I presume. Care to tell me who that is on the ground outside with my partner?"

"My brother," Luisa said, casting her eyes down at the ground in shame but then a second later lifting them. She was defiant but also afraid, like she didn't know whether to hope for the best or scream out the window for him to try to run again. "Please. He didn't have any choice but to come here. There are men back where I came from, they're trying to hurt him and…"

Laura held up a hand, cutting her off. "Your brother is here illegally," she said. It was half statement, half question.

"Yes," Luisa said, her cheeks burning now. There was still that spark of fight in her eyes. "Please. I'm telling you, if you send him back he will die. They won't listen. The—the immigration people. I just wanted to keep him safe. Please, don't send him back."

Laura watched her evenly for a moment. "We'll talk about that in a moment," she said. "You've missed your shifts at the Great Maple Ohio Hotel for the last couple of days."

Luisa nodded. "I needed to stay home to help Jorge." She stopped and frowned. "Why is my missing work a matter for the FBI?"

"It isn't," Laura said, narrowing her eyes slightly. The maid had a good reason for not going to work the past couple of days. Was it just a coincidence that she had started helping her brother out at the same time the murders started? "I need to talk to you about a couple of guests that stayed in the hotel last month. You cleaned their rooms. Let me show you their images." She dug her cell phone out of her pocket and held it up, showing her first Michaels and then Bluton.

Luisa frowned, shaking her head. "Maybe I did, maybe not," she said. "I couldn't say for certain. I don't get to see many of the guests—they're usually out when I go in to clean up."

"Do you always work when you're scheduled, until the last couple of days?" Laura asked.

"Yes, of course!" Luisa said, then lowered her eyes. "I guess I can see why you would ask."

"Then it's very likely you were the one who cleaned their rooms," Laura insisted. There was a clatter in the hallway; she looked up to see a bedraggled and defeated-looking man who shared many of his features with Luisa. He was walking into the apartment with Agent Moore behind him, flushed but seemingly very pleased with herself. She closed the door behind them, leaving just the four of them in on the conversation. "Do you remember anything unusual from around that time? For example, a room that clearly hadn't been used or slept in even though it was booked for the night?"

Luisa shook her head. "Nothing like that. But I don't have time always to stop and think about whether something is unusual. I do so many rooms every day. Especially last month. We were so busy with all the visitors for that big gathering."

Laura frowned. "Big gathering?"

"Yeah, at the convention hall across the street from the hotel," Luisa said. Her eyes kept glancing fearfully toward Jorge, like she couldn't focus on the conversation anymore now that he was in the room. For his part, he was sweating, looking back at her like he was trying to send a message of goodbye and thanks and who knew what else all at the same time. "There was a big event going on. Most of our guests were booked in for that. It's the busiest we've ever been. I think a lot of them were making the bookings together on purpose, so they could all stay in the same place."

Laura tapped her index finger against her mouth thoughtfully. This was all starting to go somewhere.

Luisa had an alibi for the last couple of days, it seemed—though not one that would ever stand up in a court of law. She was so petite that there was no chance she had been the one to wield the knife, or whatever it was. Her brother looked stronger, tougher—but also travel-worn and grimy. If he'd come here illegally, smuggled in by a coyote with no more than the clothes on his back... they would have been covered in blood.

She was making a lot of assumptions, she knew. But she felt something in her gut.

If they let this man go, he probably wouldn't be here when they came back. It was on her head if she made a mistake.

"Do you recognize these people?" she asked, on a whim, swinging her phone screen up to the level of Jorge's eyeline. His eyes flicked to the picture automatically, and Laura scrolled, watching him. Behind her, Luisa translated what she had said into rapid-fire Spanish. Laura knew enough to know she hadn't added anything or warned him to be quiet.

He shook his head no, a confused expression on his face. Laura had been watching him closely. There wasn't even a flicker of recognition, fear, anger—anything that would have given him away as the killer.

"Take off his cuffs," she told Agent Moore, putting her phone away. "We're done here."

"You're letting him go?" Luisa asked, her voice full of hope.

Laura nodded curtly. She couldn't get involved, not really. They had still broken the law. But the good news was that it wasn't her department. She was there to solve a murder, nothing else.

"We're not here for that," Laura said. She tilted her head toward the door when Agent Moore gave her a questioning look. "Come on. We'd better get to that convention center."

"Right," Agent Moore said, scrambling to shove her cuffs back away and head to the door.

"Miss Lopez," Laura added, pausing in the doorway. She found suddenly she couldn't quite meet their eyes. "That conversation we just had was a little loud at the start. You might want to seek accommodations elsewhere by the end of the day—at least for your brother. Otherwise, people might be here asking questions that aren't so easy to answer."

She tapped the doorframe by way of farewell and left, uttering an unspoken prayer in her head that the residents of the building were too apathetic to bother calling ICE before they'd driven away.

CHAPTER THIRTEEN

Laura felt like she was going in circles already. First the hotel, then the apartment building where they'd found Luisa and Jorge, and now back outside the hotel again.

"Are we really allowed to do that, though?" Agent Moore asked for what felt like the sixteenth time. "Just let him go?"

Laura sighed. "Are you going to personally call ICE and let them know?"

"No," Agent Moore said, looking horrified. "Of course not."

"Are you going to tell Rondelle when we get back that I didn't arrest someone who broke the law?"

"No," Agent Moore said, more hesitantly. "But—"

"Then who's to stop me from doing it?" Laura asked. She switched off the engine. "We're here. Stop thinking about what happened back there and get your head back in the game. We're too busy tracking down a double murderer to worry about immigration issues."

"Right," Agent Moore replied, though less convincingly than Laura would have liked.

Truth be told, she knew as she got out of the rental car that there was a chance she could get into a lot of trouble for what she'd done. She had knowingly allowed someone to continue staying in the country illegally. As much as her own feelings on the matter might be that it wasn't worth ruining someone's life over, the law was the law.

She was relying on the rookie to be too awed by Laura's seniority to let it happen without mentioning it to anyone who had the power to do something about it. She was also, maybe, hoping that the rookie would pick up on the act of altruism and learn to do the same.

If he wasn't harming anyone, then there was no reason for Laura to be involved in any way in the matter of whether he should be allowed to stay or forced to return where he had come from.

The convention hall was easy enough to find—Laura had noticed it on their way in earlier. It stood directly opposite the hotel as Luisa had suggested. It was very likely that the one had been built to service the other, knowing that a lot of out-of-towners might be looking for a place to stay. Laura shaded her eyes as she looked up at it. It was big, considering what a small town they were in. It wasn't much more populous than the farming town they had driven over from. But the convention center was clearly a draw for people from all over the county, if not the state.

Laura walked over from the hotel to the center, knowing that if she was right, she was walking in the footsteps of their victims. If they had both stayed at the hotel and both visited a convention, that didn't necessarily mean they weren't having an affair. But it did hint at a different connection between them—some kind of shared interest or possibly a career.

Not that they seemed, on the surface, to be working in the same field—but perhaps Janae Michaels had been in training.

"Do you recall seeing anything in their bank statements about this?" Laura asked, looking over her shoulder. "Any ticket purchase?"

Agent Moore shook her head, stumbling a little as she rushed over to catch up. "No, nothing," she said. "Maybe it was a free event? Or they paid cash at the door?"

"Possibly," Laura said. They reached the impressive double doors that led into the convention hall, and Laura hesitated for a moment. It seemed closed. What did you do? Knock, or just try to head in?

In the end, she tried the door. It opened easily, allowing them into a small lobby area with desks on both sides, no doubt set up to speed up the entrance process.

"Hello?" she called out, loud, into the space. Her own voice echoed back to her for a moment, but the sound of movement off to one side alerted her that they were not alone. A man emerged from a side door behind one of the desks, peeking out to see who was there.

"We're closed today," he said. He was probably about twenty-five, Caucasian, with hair that was long enough to be tied into a small ponytail right at the back of his head. "If you're looking to book tickets, you can visit our website—"

"We're not customers," Laura interrupted.

"Oh, right," the man said, straightening slightly. "Well, if you want to book the hall—"

"And not clients either," Laura said. She held up her badge. "We need to ask you some questions about a convention that took place last month."

His eyes bulged. They flicked to one side, and Laura sensed that Agent Moore was also holding up her own badge. "What's this about? We haven't done anything wrong, have we? I'm just the marketing manager, so I don't—"

"Is that the office?" Laura asked, clapping her hands together meaningfully and rubbing her palms together. "It sure would be nice to be invited in out of the cold to sit and have a coffee."

The man cleared his throat, nodding his understanding. "Right. Would you like to come inside?"

"Thanks so much," Laura grinned, breezing past the desk and following him through to the office on the other side. It was a small space—only a collection of four desks, three of them pushed together with one at the head, probably belonging to the boss of the company. There was no one else inside. "Is everyone else home today?"

"We tend to take our vacation time on days when there's nothing on in the hall," the marketing manager said. "I drew the short straw, I guess. We like to have someone in to answer the phones, at least."

Laura sat down behind one of the desks at random, noting that it held a collection of ceramic cat figurines in miniature around the monitor and keyboard. "So. Last month's schedule?" she asked.

"Um," he said, running a hand back over his hair. One of the strands caught in a ring he was wearing and fell loose from his ponytail. "I guess… we started off with a symposium on new farming techniques. We have a lot of those, actually. There was a sci-fi convention. It's a bit of a quiet month—after that we had a break for a few days, and then we had this ancestors reunion thing, and then another break before the medical equipment fair—"

"What was that one—the ancestors reunion?" Laura asked, frowning. Something about the name had struck a chord with her. It wasn't a vision—just the more old-fashioned kind of detective work, going with her gut.

The marketing manager shuffled some papers on another desk and pulled out a glossy flyer. "Here—it's kind of a trend that seems to be happening lately. People get together with everyone who shares a common ancestor with them. It's like a family reunion, but, like, much bigger."

Laura studied the poster. She handed it to Agent Moore, who had taken the desk opposite her, without a word. The dates listed at the bottom of the page matched exactly with the dates that both Janae Michaels and James Bluton had stayed at the hotel.

Still, that wasn't quite proof. Not yet.

"Can I see your attendee records?" Laura asked. "We need to see if the people we're investigating were there."

"Sure, I have them in a database on my computer," he said. He fidgeted awkwardly where he stood, brushing his hand back over his hair again. "Um… it's just, you're in my seat."

Laura looked at the collection of cat figurines and then back at him with a raised eyebrow. When all he could do was shrug apologetically, she sighed, got up, and moved out of his way so that he could sit down. The advantage now, of course, was that she could look over his shoulder at the computer screen.

She could also see the office's coffee machine at this angle—and it looked like a very fancy machine indeed, the kind that would make coffee you actually enjoyed drinking rather than just throwing it back.

"Agent Moore," she said. "Why don't you get us that coffee?"

If she was honest, she was expecting resistance. But Agent Moore simply leapt up out of her chair with an enthusiastic nod and scurried over to the machine, grabbing a couple of mugs from a display right next to it.

"Okay," the marketing manager said. Laura had watched him log in. His name was Ben. "I have the database up and ready. What's the name you need to check?"

"There are two," Laura said. "Janae Michaels and James Bluton."

"Can you spell that surname?" he asked, typing in as she read out the letters to him. After a moment, he nodded with satisfaction and pointed at the screen. "There we go—there's your James Bluton. Attended both days. And… yep, the same for Janae Michaels. They were both here for both days of the event."

They'd both been there.

Laura allowed herself a small smile of victory. They had their link. Whatever it was that made the killer target them, it had something to do with this ancestors reunion. Which meant it was almost certain the killer was someone who had also attended. Perhaps an argument had taken place, or they had witnessed something they weren't supposed to.

"Can we verify that absolutely?" Laura asked. "Surveillance footage of the front desk, perhaps?"

Ben shrugged. "I can get it for you. I don't know how clearly we'll be able to see them—I know it was a busy day."

"How busy could it possibly have been?" Laura asked. "This is just people who are related, right?"

"Yeah, but they're distantly related—like fourth, fifth, sixth cousins and beyond. Most of the attendees never even meet before the day of the reunion," Ben said. "It starts a few generations back. If you think about the possibilities—children and children's children and children's children's children, and so on, you end up with a lot of people coming in through the doors."

"How many?" Laura asked in alarm. From the other side of the room there was a large hiss of steam, seeming to punctuate her words.

"Looks like we had one thousand, nine hundred and eighty-nine people in attendance," Ben said, clicking back to the main list on his database.

Laura just gaped at him.

"Um," Agent Moore said, calling their attention back to her. She had a kind of upset look on her face. She reminded Laura of a puppy that thought it was about to get told off and really wished it could avoid it. "I think I broke your coffee machine."

"What?" Ben asked, jumping to his feet.

Laura was similarly upset; she'd been looking forward to that coffee. "It can't be that bad," she said. "You probably just didn't press the right button."

"No, no," Ben said, bending over the machine. "Looks like she's managed to pull out one of the components. The wires are all loose. This is going to need to go back to the manufacturer to be fixed!"

"Oh dear," Laura said, her tone flat but hurried. "Terribly sorry. If you could just print out that list for us and give us the name of the organizer?"

"Give me a minute," Ben said, rubbing his face. "The boss is going to kill me. This thing cost more than my car."

"Let me see if I can fix it," Agent Moore said, her tone one of complete panic. She turned to fiddle with something on the back of the coffee machine—

And the room plunged into total darkness, with a whirring noise as every electrical item in the place powered down.

"What did you touch?!" Ben demanded, clearly very distressed about what his boss was going to say now.

"That name, and we'll get out of your hair," Laura suggested. "I promise Agent Moore won't touch anything else."

Agent Moore made a kind of squeak in the darkness, as if to say that she agreed to the terms.

"It's on my desk," Ben said, his voice having risen at least an octave in stress. "Just... let me..." He moved through the room, swearing when he bumped into the corner of a desk, and then flipped the screen of his cell phone on to illuminate his desk. He shuffled through what looked like scrap paper to find the torn-off edge of something and thrust it at Laura.

"Many thanks," she said, as cheerfully as she could. "Well, goodbye then!"

She made a beeline for the exit, making sure to grab Agent Moore by the arm on the way past and haul her out before she could do any more damage.

CHAPTER FOURTEEN

Nate sat at his desk in the J. Edgar Hoover Building—the FBI headquarters. He was supposed to be clearing it out. After the incident on the bridge, he'd been given a couple of weeks' paid leave to help him deal with it—not that he really needed to.

Not with the attempt on his life, anyway. The revelation about Laura was maybe different.

So, he was supposed to finish his leave and then make his transfer. It was almost all completed. All he had to do was sign the paperwork and clear out his desk. The paperwork was in a manila folder which he had carefully carried in from his car and laid down on his desk, right next to the cardboard box with the sides folded in that he intended to use for his things.

Now that he was sitting here, though, it didn't all seem so easy.

He just had to move his damn arms and pick up everything one by one. Pick it up and put it in the box. How hard could that be?

And yet, here he found himself. Staring instead of moving. Lost in thought.

It had started with the rest of the paperwork in his in tray. He'd picked it up and placed it in front of him, on top of the folder. He figured maybe he should fill it all out and then hand it in to Rondelle at the same time, save himself having to make the trip upstairs more than once. But then he'd actually read it. It was related to a case he and Laura had worked before—one they'd solved together. They'd saved lives then. Now the court was asking for an update on the evidence trail of a certain object that had been used in the murders, and they needed him to fill out and sign an affidavit on that front.

It had brought it all back, seeing the paperwork. Nate sat there and remembered what they had done. The last victim, a girl no older than ten—they'd found her just in time to free her. She'd been traumatized, of course, but she was still alive. They'd done that.

But now, looking back, he realized the truth. *Laura* had done that.

They had been racing against time and stuck up a creek without a paddle. Spinning in circles trying to catch a killer who didn't seem to leave any trace of himself behind. But then out of nowhere, Laura had had this idea to look into connections with the local school. They hadn't been looking in that area at all—the victims had been older. They didn't even come from the same schools. But it turned out there was one man who had worked at both, and he'd worked in education for twenty years, meaning he'd come across all of the victims one way or another in the school halls.

Laura had put it together from luck, she said, and gut instinct, and a random thought about the school that had led her in the right direction. She'd even said that Nate probably would have gotten there himself if he'd been given enough time. But now he understood the truth: she'd had some kind of vision which led her to the killer.

It had all been down to the visions—almost every success they'd ever had. Maybe even the ones that Nate didn't suspect.

All the times he'd thought they worked on it together. What, was she feeding him information?

Was he even that good of an agent, like he had thought he was all this time? Or was it all down to Laura?

He'd had successes before they were partnered together, but... all the cases that had made their names as the top agents they were had been together. All of them. Would he have even gotten this far in his career if it wasn't for her visions?

Everything was starting to make sense to him. All of her hunches, her gut feelings, her instincts. He'd teased her about it plenty of times. There were times when he'd been suspicious, even accused her of having secret informants. Or worse. Mob ties, or something. He hadn't known what to think.

But that hadn't been until late in their relationship. They'd been partners for a really long time before he even started to doubt that she just had a killer instinct. Pun intended.

He'd been so dumb, all this time.

He was supposed to be an FBI agent. The people the cops turned to when they couldn't figure out a case. How had he been letting this happen under his nose for all this time without noticing it?

And when she'd told him—oh, man. When she'd told him, he'd thought she was crazy. Losing her mind. He'd told her to get psychiatric help. It was a miracle she'd even shown up to stop him getting pushed off the bridge.

But hell, what a way to prove to him that she was the real deal.

"Hey, Nate!"

He looked up, startled. He'd almost forgotten he wasn't alone. With Laura's desk—right in front of his—conspicuously empty, he'd felt cut off from the rest of the guys in the bullpen. But Freddie Jones, one of the agents who sat right behind them, was just coming back to his desk with lunch.

"Freddie," he said, feeling like he'd just woken up from a deep sleep. "How's it going?"

"Good, man, good." Freddie nodded. The guy was a little too enthusiastic sometimes, in a sweet kind of way. He had a son he adored, and he was always great with kids when they came in—reassuring, kind, fatherly. Now, though, he was frowning. "It's not true, is it? You're leaving us for a local branch?"

"Uh." Nate paused, looking down. He didn't know how to answer that. Not really. "Well, I just have to finish the paperwork. It's not a done deal until then."

Freddie tsked, sitting down on the edge of Nate's desk. "Don't do it. I know you and Laura fell out lately, and I don't know what it was about, but you two are good together. Don't throw it all away, Nate. Try and make it work."

Nate's mouth quirked up at one side in amusement. "We're not married."

"I know," Freddie said, rolling his eyes. "But real partnership like that is hard to find, even here. You're a great team. You have a better record than just about anyone else in this place, and you know it's only because you always get paired up. Laura can't hold onto another partner to save her life. If you go, it's going to be back to the revolving doors again."

Nate frowned slightly. "Revolving doors?"

"New partner every case," Freddie said. "And the more she gets put with new people, the more prickly she gets. You know she hates babysitting the rookies, but those are the only agents that will work with her."

"Why? She's a good agent. Easy to work with. What don't they like?"

"They find her a little weird." Freddie shrugged. "Anyway, see? You do like her, really."

Nate sighed. He did. He did like working with Laura. He missed her, too. But it was a lot to take in—this psychic thing. He didn't even know how far it went. Did she have visions of him when he was at home on his own? Did she see bits of his private life that he would rather keep separate from work?

And what was he supposed to do with all this new knowledge? Keep it secret for her?

70

Would he have to lie to their superiors—to Rondelle? On legal documents? In court?

It would be so much easier if people knew what she could do. She wouldn't be weird—she'd be an asset. But then, he guessed there were negative sides to that coin, and it was her choice to make. Still, why hadn't she ever tried to go public with it?

Nate sighed again. "Yeah," he said, getting up. "Anyway. I'm going for lunch. See you later, Freddie."

He had to get out of here. Before he could hand over the paperwork, before he could clear his desk, he needed answers.

It just sucked that the only one who could provide them was Laura.

CHAPTER FIFTEEN

"Who is she, then?" Laura asked, leaning forward slightly to check the road in both directions before pulling out.

"Looks like she's some kind of genealogist," Agent Moore replied thoughtfully, scrolling through the results on her phone. "She's organized quite a few of these ancestors reunion things. She tends to keep them local, I suppose so she can always attend and make sure everything runs smoothly. There are loads of testimonials and galleries from past events on her website."

"Anything about our event?"

"Not much yet. It was recent, so I suppose she hasn't processed it correctly. There's a small gallery, but not as many shots as the others."

Laura glanced her way before focusing back on the road. "Any shots of our victims?"

Agent Moore was silent for a moment, scrolling. "No," she said, at length. "Not yet."

"That's a good thing," Laura pointed out. "It means that we know the killer must have attended in person. If he didn't, he would have no way to know who attended and who didn't. Well, unless he had access to the guest list, of course—we can ask her about that when we arrive. What was her name again, Alice…?"

"Alice Papadopoli," Agent Moore replied, the name rattling off her tongue naturally. "She doesn't have any opening hours listed on her website. What if she's not in when we get there?"

"Then we'll try to get a home address," Laura said. Her hands flexed on the steering wheel in frustration at a slower vehicle blocking their way. It felt like all they'd done since getting up this morning was drive around from one place to another. She was hoping that this Papadopoli would be in the office listed on her website—because if she wasn't, it would only mean another agonizing delay.

"This is so interesting," Agent Moore said, lost in whatever she had found on the site. "Do you think I have distant cousins out there who I've never met?"

"That's how it works," Laura said, her impatience almost boiling over as they stopped at a red light, fingers tapping on the wheel. "Everyone has distant cousins they've never met."

"Everyone?" Agent Moore asked, thinking about it. "I haven't met my close cousins, come to think about it. I never got a chance. When we were living in the commune, it was just us. Actually, I thought our neighbors were my cousins for years, but that was just because we were supposed to call all older adults Aunt and Uncle. They weren't really related to me at all."

What an odd life Agent Moore had had. Laura didn't say it. Even if she wasn't sure that Agent Moore would even realize it was rude to say so. "You say she's organized a lot of these things, but always here? It's a bit random, isn't it?"

"Well, not if she lives here," Agent Moore said.

"It doesn't matter where *she* lives," Laura said. "You'd think it would be easier to hold this kind of thing in a big city. Or at least, near one. Everyone who attends has to come out to the middle of nowhere. Why would she do it like that?"

Agent Moore shrugged silently. Glancing over from the corner of her eye, Laura realized she probably didn't even know that traveling to a rural location for a random conference hall wasn't unusual. She probably didn't understand the concept of distant relations being scattered all across the country, to the extent that many of them might have needed to fly in. To make that possible, surely you'd want to hold your reunion near major transport links—an airport, a train station, a metro system.

"I think it's nice," Agent Moore said, as Laura took another turn. "Imagine meeting all those people you're related to that you didn't even know! I wish someone would organize one for my ancestors."

"I've never heard of one of these before," Laura mused. "Never been invited to one. It seems unlikely, doesn't it? If she's done so many of them, eventually you do get to a point where everyone is connected."

"Are you sad you've missed out as well?" Agent Moore asked. "Maybe we can ask her if she can check our DNA and organize something!"

Laura shook her head impatiently as she pulled up outside the office indicated by her GPS. It was clearly a shared space—an old warehouse converted into offices, with a dozen company signs out front. None of them were for this genealogist. "I mean, what if these other events are faked, and the whole point of this convention was to get certain people in a room with one another? Maybe to lure them somehow or push them together? Let me look at that website."

Agent Moore handed her cell phone over—Laura noticing as she did that it was an older model, with a bit of damage to the bottom corner of the screen—and she looked at the site closely. She scrolled through the pages, speed-reading each one as well as she could. There wasn't anything she could see that would definitively guarantee the events were real. She checked the photos from a recent event, noting the quality was better than the ones from the one their victims had attended, and her thumb hit an image of the organizer as she scrolled, sending a jolt of pain through her temple and—

The same farmers, the ones she had seen before. They were standing around in the same configuration, talking silently. There wasn't a sound between them, even though their mouths were moving. It was like Laura was deaf.

The same vision again. What was she supposed to gain from this, except for knowing she was on the right path?

Laura watched, unable to control the vision, impatient for it to end. If this wasn't going to show her anything new, it was a waste of her—

One of the farmers turned, his face wide in a scream, his eyes open in panic. She couldn't hear what he was saying, but he was running, and she followed him. She couldn't see the others. She only saw him running through the field, racing away as fast as he could, from—someone? Something?

Laura blinked, the images on the phone still moving in the scroll she had initiated. They hit the bottom of the gallery and she handed it back to Agent Moore, trying to ignore the light throbbing in her head. It was easy enough. She'd spent her life ignoring the pounding pain of immediate visions, not the light throb of this view into the past.

"Well," she said. "Better go inside."

She watched Agent Moore get out of the car, giving herself a moment of breathing space. She had to figure out what she had seen. The farmers were running and screaming—clearly, something had frightened them. But who, or what? And what did that have to do with what was happening now?

If she had been in a Hollywood blockbuster, she would have assumed that some kind of nightmarish creature was back after two hundred years to exact its revenge on the people who persecuted it before. But this wasn't a movie, and that kind of curse wasn't real. Even if she had psychic powers, it still didn't make her believe in witches, ghosts, and ghouls.

So, what could possibly connect early American farmers with the modern-day killings?

She had a feeling she was going to need far more than one vision to find out—but with no way to trigger them except to keep investigating,

74

she got out of the car, following Agent Moore up to the office building's front door. There was a buzzer panel beside it, so they had no choice but to press the button which had Alice Papadopoli listed beside it and wait for her to let them in.

"Hello?"

"Ms. Papadopoli, this is the FBI. Can we come in and speak to you? It's regarding one of your events," Laura said, keeping her words as neutral as possible. The more serious she knew the case was, the more likely their genealogist would try to run.

"Uh, yes. Please come up." There was a buzz, and the door clicked; pushing it, Laura found it open, and stepped inside.

They crossed a tiny lobby scattered with old junk mail that had drifted in through the door and then been left to pile up, climbing a grimy staircase to the first floor. Laura began to have serious misgivings as they passed under a flickering lightbulb to knock on the door marked with the name they were looking for. What kind of office was this? It didn't look like a place where someone with a legitimate business would set themselves up.

She knocked on the door and it flew open before she had even finished the gesture, revealing an older woman in a thin cardigan over a densely patterned floral dress. She was tiny, with bone-like arms and legs that immediately put Laura in mind of a fragile bird.

"Hello," she said. "I'm Alice Papadopoli."

"Ms. Papadopoli," Laura responded, blinking. "I am Special Agent Laura Frost, and this is my partner, Agent Bee Moore."

"Be more what?" Alice asked, without missing a beat.

"Be more everything," Agent Moore replied, grinning wide. "Anything that you are. Just be more."

Alice laughed merrily and turned to allow them in. Agent Moore followed her with almost a skip in her step, leaving Laura to shake her head wordlessly and follow once both of them could no longer see her.

At least it had worked, in terms of getting them inside.

"What's all this about?" Alice asked, perching on a chair behind the one desk in the tiny office. There was just enough room for a couple of chairs opposite her, and Laura and Agent Moore both sank into one of these. "You mentioned my events?"

"Yes," Laura said, reaching into her pocket. She drew out the poster she had taken from the marketing manager at the conference hall, smoothing it out where she had folded it. "This one, in particular. It took place just last month."

Alice took the paper and nodded, her large head bobbing up and down in the air on what seemed an impossibly long neck. Her fingers were thin except around the knuckles, where they bulged in bony outcroppings; Laura suspected arthritis. "Ah, yes. This was very special. What is it that you want to know about it?"

"Why was it special?" Laura asked with a frown. That wasn't the kind of response she had expected, and it was a good place to start.

"Well, because this was my own reunion," Alice said with a beam. "I've organized them for a few other clients in the past, but this time, I decided to look into my own ancestry. It turned out I could trace my lineage back quite a way in the local area, through several different branches that started with the original Michaels family. And, wouldn't you know it? There were thousands of us. Hundreds and hundreds still in the state. I decided I just had to go ahead and host an event for all of my long-lost distant relatives."

It was clear from the way she spoke that she was very proud of the event and the way it had gone. "Everyone there was a relative of yours?" Laura said, because she had to be absolutely certain.

"Yes! Even the security at the door." Alice grinned. "Actually, that wasn't planned—it just so turned out that a couple of people who already did a bit of part-time work at the convention hall were part of the right gene pool. Just another bit of fate that made me feel I'd made the right choice in setting the event up!"

"Oh, how lovely!" Agent Moore gushed. "Imagine that, having every single person you see be a relative of yours. It must have been magical!"

"It really was," Alice said, with a confessing tone to her voice. "I now know what it feels like for my clients, which was quite the surprise. I didn't expect it to be so emotional—or so rewarding."

"Could you tell me where you were yesterday, and the day before?" Laura asked, cutting across their touching conversation to get to the point.

Alice looked up sharply at the change in direction. "Where I was? Well, yesterday I was here in the office for most of the day. I had a few client meetings. And the day before I took the day off to go and visit my sister, since I didn't have anything booked—she's just moved into a residential facility a couple of hours away, and I wanted to make sure she was settling in properly."

"They'll have you logged in and out as a guest, won't they?" Laura asked, raising her eyebrows.

"Yes, I guess so." Alice nodded. "What is this about?"

Laura took out her notebook and placed it in front of her. "We'll need the name of that facility so we can check with them," she said, even though she didn't really think that there was any question of Alice being their murderer. She was far too thin and frail-looking, and with those hands, Laura wondered if she could even wield a knife. She watched Alice write the name with satisfaction, noting it was difficult for her to even hold a pen. "I'm afraid there have been two murders which we believe might have been linked to the reunion."

Alice jumped, nearly dropping the pen. Her face went white. "No," she breathed. "That can't be. Who was killed?"

Laura opened up the images of Janae Michaels and Jamie Bluton on her phone. "Do you recognize them?"

"Yes!" Alice exclaimed, but then her face colored slightly. "I don't remember their names—you'll have to forgive me, there were so many people—but they were definitely at the event!"

"That's okay," Agent Moore spoke up. "I forget people's names all the time! I got introduced to my new colleagues for the first time recently, and I'd forgotten all of them by the time we went around the room."

Alice chuckled. "Yes, well, my memory's not what it used to be, either."

"Do you remember hearing of any disputes or disagreements at the event?" Laura asked. "Anything negative at all that could explain why this has happened?"

"No," Alice said, the corners of her mouth dropping down in pure misery. "No, it was a wonderful event and everyone had so much fun. Or, so I thought. Now, I don't know what to think."

"Do you have a list of everyone who attended the event?" Laura asked. They still needed one, after all. The marketing manager hadn't been able to provide it for them before Agent Moore managed to kill the power, and there was no telling when he would be able to get it back up and running or get access to that database remotely. Laura shot a subtle glance down at Agent Moore's hands to make sure they were firmly and safely placed on her lap.

"I do," Alice said. "And everyone who was invited. Which do you want?"

Laura blinked. "Both," she said. That was much more useful than she had expected. They might actually be able to make sense of something if they had data from both lists.

Although, the only time it would probably come in handy would be if someone else died, and they were only on the invited list, not the

77

attended list—which was a depressing thought. But then she shook her head. The first two victims had actually attended, so that wouldn't be a link.

"I'll help as much as I can," Alice said, as her printer whirred into life. Laura had a flashback to the previous office they were in and held her breath, but it soon started spurting out page after page of names and she relaxed.

Until she realized the enormity of what they were dealing with.

The marketing manager had said there were almost two thousand people in attendance. There were even more who were invited, but chose not to attend.

They had a lot of potential suspects—and a lot of potential future victims.

The problem was, Laura wasn't sure what she was supposed to do next.

And Agent Moore was looking at her in that way that made it absolutely clear that Laura was going to have to be the one to decide.

CHAPTER SIXTEEN

As they left the dilapidated office building, Laura rubbed a hand over her forehead in frustration. It had gotten dark while they were in there. It was getting later in the evening, and they still really had nothing.

Well, they had something. Two thousand names and counting. And she wasn't sure there was any way to narrow down the list other than to start interviewing people who had attended and seeing if they knew anything or had alibis to rule them out. Even warning them to be safe was going to take days with the kind of manpower they had, and a television appeal at this point would just create mass panic.

"Are we going back to the inn now?" Agent Moore asked. "I spoke to them this morning and they said that they can provide dinner, but only until eleven. And it's only cooked fresh until nine—after that, they just reheat whatever was left over from everyone else. We should try to get back before then."

Laura sighed. It was late, yes, but she always hated giving up and going to bed for the night. Especially these days. The longer they stayed here, the more likely it was that she was going to miss her weekend visit with her daughter, Lacey, yet again. And there was so much at home that waited for her. She still needed to speak to Nate. She wanted to go on another date with Chris. She wanted to sleep in her own bed, not the strangely claustrophobia-inducing rooms of the inn.

She wanted to be home as soon as possible, and going to bed early—not that it was really early anymore—wouldn't help that.

But on the other hand, she didn't have a lot of options.

She was about to ask Agent Moore to take the wheel when she remembered the rookie's story about only recently learning to drive and rethought the idea. "Can you make a few calls to the office back home while I drive?" she asked. "We need to get some extra eyes on this data. There's no way the two of us are going to be able to get through all of those names on our own."

"Sure," Agent Moore agreed easily. "What do we need?"

"First thing we're going to need is a way to transfer that data," Laura said. "Shoot. I should have asked her to email me a copy of those printouts. Hold on, I'll go back up—"

"It's fine," Agent Moore said. "I saw a fax machine in the inn's back office."

Laura thought about asking what Agent Moore had been doing in the back office, but she thought better of it. There was probably some kooky explanation involving her having grown up in a commune, and she didn't have time for it. "Okay, great. We can get it back to them that way. You need to call up HQ and get the techs on board with some searches."

"What are they looking for?"

Laura glanced over and saw Agent Moore was writing everything down in her notebook. "Anyone with a criminal record or a known history of mental illness," she said. "We can at least start there. These attacks are brutal. I would guess that our perpetrator either has psychotic issues, or has done this before—maybe starting small with knife crimes or less violent attacks."

"How do we want that sent back to us?"

"As emails," Laura said immediately. "Name, address if known, and anything relevant about their history. Ask them to work on it through the night, if we can. That way we'll have the data available when we wake up in the morning. First thing, by the way. I want to be able to hit the ground running as soon as possible."

"What about just local attendees?" Agent Moore asked. "That way we could narrow it down a lot more."

"Right, but we don't really have enough data at this point to be sure the killer will stay local," Laura said. "Or that he hasn't traveled here from out of state, maybe using the convention as an excuse to scope out the area first time around. We can't make a mistake by narrowing it down too quickly on faulty assumptions, no matter how tempting that may seem."

"I'll give them a call right now," Agent Moore said, setting down her pen and picking up her cell phone.

Laura drove back to the little inn, a couple of hours away from the town they had ended up searching in, while she listened to Agent Moore making the calls. She chimed in a few times where it was needed, letting the younger woman know what details she had missed or which pieces of terminology she needed. Half her brain was focused on the road, and the other half on the conversation.

Well, most of the time.

Because every now and then she would drift out of paying attention and into thinking about her own life and the things that always came to the surface when she had a moment of breathing space from whatever case she was working on.

"That's it for the night, then?" Agent Moore asked, as they pulled up outside the inn. "We'll eat and then go to bed?"

"Yes," Laura replied, though she wished she could skip the dinner part altogether. She had too many things on her mind, and her stomach was roiling when she thought about food. Mostly, she thought about the glass of wine that might easily accompany a nice meal. The glass of wine they would probably be offered.

She hoped she had the strength to turn it down.

Agent Moore went to get out of the car, and Laura made a quick motion that arrested her momentum. "Just keep your mind alert and ready for whatever might happen," she said. "If we get a call that there's been another body in the middle of the night, we'll be getting up and rushing out to it. Don't let yourself settle in too much—and definitely no alcohol with dinner. Right?"

"Right," Agent Moore said, and Laura breathed a sigh of relief to herself. It was a bit deceitful, to pretend it was the rookie who needed to watch what she drank, but at least this would help Laura to stay on the straight and narrow as well.

"I'm going to my room to make a couple of personal calls," Laura said. "I'll see you down there in half an hour."

Agent Moore nodded again, getting out of the car for real this time. She pushed the door shut behind her and soon disappeared inside the inn—a picture of countryside sweetness with rambling plants climbing trellises across red brickwork, and a porch set up with various tables and loungers for breakfast in the summers.

Laura looked away, got out of the car, and forced herself to head upstairs and do as she'd said she would. She wanted to talk to someone. To anyone, really, but to someone in particular.

Well, if she was honest with herself, she wanted to talk to Nate.

That wasn't an option, though, was it? After the way they had left things, she didn't know if he would even pick up. And if he did, he probably wouldn't welcome her hounding him like that. He'd made it clear that he needed time and space. He needed to be away from her.

Even after she'd saved his life, and he knew it.

Laura shook her head in the solitude of her room. The stuffy furniture and fussy floral bedspread almost seemed to mock her. So domestic and rural and sweet; exactly the opposite of what she was.

She couldn't stand it.

She picked up her phone and dialed Chris's number without letting herself think about it too much, waiting impatiently for it to connect.

"Laura!" he exclaimed, sounding as if he had been waiting for her call all along. "How's it going on your case?"

Laura closed her eyes and threw herself backwards onto the chintzy covers on the bed. "Honestly? Not great."

"Oh, no," Chris said, with what sounded like real feeling. "Is there anything I can help with?"

"Not really," Laura sighed. Why had she even called him? Just to hear his voice, she supposed. "I'm not supposed to give any details on open cases to civilians, you understand."

"Oh, I totally get it," Chris said. "It's like doctor-patient confidentiality. You can't tell anyone the details until after it's done, and maybe not even then. Don't worry. I'll never ask you for things you're not allowed to tell."

"Right, I guess it is pretty similar," Laura said. That, in many ways, was a relief. Marcus, her ex-husband, had hated that she couldn't talk to him about her cases. She took her job seriously, and she knew that any kind of information leak could result in a mistrial and see someone she'd worked hard on taking down go free. He'd swung between trying to get her to tell him all the juicy gossip about cases that ended up in the news and not caring about her job at all.

Chris, she already knew, was different.

"So, is there anything on your mind that you can say? You need to vent some frustration?" Chris asked.

Laura passed a hand over her eyes. It felt so good to be listened to. The same way the bed was supporting her tired and aching back from a long day of work, the way Chris listened to her eased the aches and pains in her mind. "Yeah, I'm just kind of stuck," she said. "I'm not used to this. I always know what to do next, even if we haven't gotten any results yet. There's always another door to knock on. But right now, with this one, I'm stuck. I have way too much data and not enough people to go through it with me, and if we miss something, we could be stuck at square one for a really long time."

Chris made a sympathetic noise. "All you can do is your best, Laura," he said. "Can you ask for more resources from your boss?"

"I wish," Laura said, stifling a huffed laugh. "The only reason I'm out here with a rookie in the first place is that there's no one else. I should still be on leave, really. Or at least doing desk work. My boss just doesn't have the bodies to send down here."

"Then you have to work with what you've got," Chris said. "It's not ideal, and it might take longer than you're used to. But so long as you're still moving forward, it's all progress, right?"

"It's just not fast enough," she said. "If I get this wrong, people can end up dead!"

"I've been there," Chris said, with some amusement in his voice.

Of course.

Now Laura felt like an idiot.

How could she have forgotten that she was talking to a cardiologist? Out of all the people she'd ever met who weren't also in law enforcement, he was probably the person who could understand what she was going through the most clearly. The responsibility of it.

"Sorry," she said. "I'm just... feeling useless."

"You're far from useless," Chris said. She could hear his warm smile in his voice. There was a faint clicking in the background, and she could picture him stirring a spoon around in his coffee. It was a picture that looked kind of like home. "If I was a criminal, I'd be terrified to hear you were on the case. You're going to get them. You always do. Just trust your instincts."

He was right. She did always get them.

He just didn't know that she had more than mere instincts to rely on.

"Thanks, Chris," she said, stifling a yawn.

"And get some rest, too," he added with a chuckle. "You must be exhausted, after yesterday."

Had it only been yesterday? It already felt like it had all happened a year ago. "Right," Laura said. "I'll, um. I'll let you know when I'm back in the state."

"I hope it's in time for the girls' day together this weekend," he said. "Good luck, Laura. Not that you need it. And goodnight."

"Goodnight," she said, with a faint smile warming her face.

Food, to refuel her body. Sleep, to refuel her brain. Then up again first thing and back at it.

They would get this guy yet. She knew it. And her instincts never let her down.

CHAPTER SEVENTEEN

Hank chuckled to himself, placing the card back on the mantelpiece. It was so lovely of them, really it was. And it had given him, old as he was, something to look forward to tomorrow.

He'd been dreading his birthdays ever since Anita passed. It always seemed like he was just another year older, another year colder. Anita had been the one to keep him warm. Their son, who was always ungrateful anyway and probably would have tried to put him in a home by now, had died at the age of forty of a heart attack, and just like that Hank was alone.

Not anymore, though. Now he had a whole extended family to brighten his days with birthday cards.

Well, only a few of them had. But still. It was more than enough for him. A month ago he'd been all alone in the world, and now all of a sudden he had people who cared about him again.

Hank took one last look at the card and then shuffled over to look at his calendar, hanging on the back of the kitchen door where Anita always liked to look at it when she was cooking. It was no use to her now, but Hank had left it there out of respect. Anita ran a good home. There was no reason for him to argue with her methods even now she was gone.

"Happy birthday, Hank old boy," he muttered to himself, eyeing tomorrow's date with glee. There it was, in his own shaky penmanship—first his birthday, etched on in block capitals the day he'd bought the calendar. Next to it, added only a week ago, the engagement: 3PM—WESTMORES—BBQ.

They were throwing him a barbecue for his birthday. He wasn't even going to have to buy any food or do any of the cleaning—they'd offered to host the whole thing, to pick him up and then drive him home afterwards. Once they'd found out he was a distant relative of theirs—a great-uncle—they'd insisted on him not spending his birthday alone, no matter how many times he told them that was usual for him now.

Thank goodness they hadn't listened.

Hank ambled over to his kitchen, their kitchen, really Anita's kitchen, and started puttering through the shelves, looking for something to eat today. He didn't have much appetite, which was fine; he wanted to save some room for tomorrow so that he could really enjoy it. He picked out a packet of mac and cheese which just needed hot water added to it, thinking that it looked just fine. Anita's voice in his head, as always, warned him that it wasn't exactly good for his heart. But he would eat it anyway, because there was no one to help out as far as more complex cooking was concerned.

As he poured the mac and cheese mix into a bowl, hard rattling shells hitting the porcelain, he glanced at his watch and saw it was past six-thirty already. Time for that blasted cat to come in and scrounge some food, if he was in the mood for it. He belonged to some little girl somewhere in the neighborhood who liked to dress him up in ribbons and sparkling collars, which the cat bore with a kind of injured dignity. He then came to Hank's back doorstep as if to say that it was past time someone repaid him for his patience, which Hank did, in the form of scraps from his table and copious ear scratches.

He moved toward the back door, listening for the telltale scratch of the cat's claws. There was nothing, but—wait—something, something different. There was a noise out there which was too big, too high, to be the cat. It had to be something bigger.

A human?

Hank frowned, moving toward the door again. What had he heard, exactly? It was cold out there, and he didn't want to have to go out for no reason—it would get into his bones, the way it wouldn't tomorrow when he could sit beside the barbecue and absorb the heat. Still, it was worth checking these things out. It was his home, after all. He didn't want someone coming in, trying to steal Anita's jewelry.

Hank moved slowly to the kitchen door, keeping an eye on the green space beyond. No sign of the cat that he could see. There was an area around to the side of the garage, where the trailing jasmine on the trellis blocked his view.

There was only one thing to do.

Hank opened the door, leaned out carefully. "Hello?" he called out. "If you're still out here, you'd better go. I've called the police already."

He paused experimentally, waiting to see if anyone would reply. Even better still, if someone would suddenly appear and jump over the fence to escape. There was nothing, however—not a single sound. Hank grunted to himself. Probably meant there hadn't been anyone out there in the first place.

Now, where was that damned cat?

A chill dropped down his spine as he considered the possibility of the third option: that someone was there, and they weren't put off by his bluff about the police, and they were just waiting to try and get inside as soon as his back was turned. Well, he wasn't going to have that.

"Mr. Fluffyhead?" he called out. He hadn't chosen the cat's name, but in that moment, he did wish he had something less ridiculous to call out. "Where are you? Come here, tsk, tsk, tsk."

No response.

Feeling a little braver, but knowing he had to prove to himself that the yard was empty before he could go back inside, Hank stepped forward. "I've got your snacks ready. Come on in, you dumb cat."

Still nothing.

"Alright," Hank called out. "I know you're not dumb. You're a very smart cat. Let's go. Time for din-dins."

He stepped forward, ready to open his mouth and call again, but—

He didn't get the chance.

Something struck him out of nowhere, quick as a flash, before he even had the chance to properly register the fact that the rest of the yard was not as empty as he had hoped. Whoever it was must have been hiding around the side of the building, behind the jasmine—it was a man, he thought—and Hank was surprised to find himself on the ground, alarmed to realize that there was pain in his chest, not sure from what.

Was he having a heart attack? He'd read a lot about heart attacks. A lot of men his age had heart attacks. Anita had always been telling him about food like that mac and cheese—

No, not a heart attack. There was blood. Where was it coming from? From his chest?

Hank looked up at the man standing over him. He was... familiar, somehow. Hank frowned, trying to put together words in his mind, trying to string together an understanding of the situation. This man. He'd seen him somewhere, hadn't he? Where had he seen him...?

He was holding something that flashed in the light of the sun—a blade—a long, tall blade—a sickle, Hank thought, grabbing the word like an anchor in the darkness and holding onto it. He held up his hands in front of his body, a silent plea.

It went unheard.

The stranger stood there, a strange expression passing over his face, something almost like a smile. Then that blade flashed down, and Hank tried to cry out but there was something wrong with his throat, and all

he could think about as he watched the sickle come down again was
that he was going to miss the barbecue after all.

CHAPTER EIGHTEEN

Laura didn't know what she had been dreaming about before, what she had done to trigger it, but there it was.

The three farmers, standing around, talking just like they always did. Calm. Not a care in the world, except maybe for their crops. Serious in that old-fashioned way, unsmiling, but not hostile. Working men with workworn hands and sun-faded clothes.

And then one of them was turning and screaming, and starting to run.

Laura half-expected things to end there, for this to be more of a recollection than a vision, a simple replay of what she had seen before. But this time she looked up again, past the man who ran and screamed, up to the two he had been with.

She saw them, too, look over their shoulders. She saw them realize what their companion had seen, their eyes going wide, their mouths falling slack with fear. She saw them turn and run, turn and chase after the first, throwing down whatever they had been holding in an effort to gain as much speed as possible. Running for their lives.

They had to be.

There was no other way to explain it—the sheer panic. They weren't running to something, the way they might go to put out a fire or save a drowning child. They were running from it, and they were terrified. Whatever it was, it was serious enough to make them think they would die if they didn't run.

Laura watched, straining, wishing as she always did that she could somehow control these visions. Like lucid dreaming. If she could only turn the "camera" around, making it look further afield, get the chance to see what was in the distance—what they were running from...

The three farmers passed out of her vision. Whatever was coming after them had to be appearing next. All she had to do was wait and she would see—

Laura's eyes snapped open on the ceiling of her room at the inn, the blaring alarm next to her not allowing her to drop back into sleep. She cursed under her breath and swiped a hand across at her phone to switch the alarm off.

She'd been so close.

She still wasn't quite convinced whether she had seen a real, bona fide vision or just a dream rehashing what she already knew, but whatever it was, it gave her equal parts frustration and hope. Frustration that she hadn't been able to see enough, yet again. Hope that this meant there was a chance she *would* see more, if she could just find a way to trigger it.

Laura sat up straight, realizing the alarm hadn't stopped. A glance at the screen showed her why: it wasn't an alarm going off at all. It was a call. She fumbled for it and answered, shoving the cell against her ear and trying to be more awake.

"Special Agent Laura Frost."

"Hi, Agent Frost, this is Sheriff Ramsgate," he said, his voice a dry crackle in the dim light of the room. She could see light coming from around the edges of the shutters. It was golden. It must be not long after dawn. "We've been alerted to another body."

"Same MO?" Laura asked, already grabbing the covers and thrusting them aside. Time to get up, to get on. The job needed her. Her heart was pounding in her chest, her stomach dropping into her feet, but there wasn't time to feel sorry for herself—to wallow in the fact that she had failed someone so badly there had been another death. What she had to do now was her absolute best to guarantee they would be the last.

"Looks like it," the Sheriff said. "I've got a deputy down at the scene now, but I'll know more when I get there myself. I'll send you the address."

"I'll be leaving in five minutes," Laura said, ending the call. She grabbed her coat, shoving her feet into her boots, and shuffled to the doorway as she tried to kick them on properly. She caught a glimpse of her face in the mirror at the side of the room above a dressing table as she passed, and tried not to look. She didn't want to face herself right now, knowing the failure that weighed heavy on her shoulders just then.

Agent Moore was sleeping in a room on the opposite side of the upstairs landing. Laura walked the few steps across to it and knocked hard on her door, then again when she heard no response.

"... Yeah?" Agent Moore's voice was sleep-bound, croaking and vaguely irritable.

"We've got another one," Laura said. "Five minutes. I'll meet you downstairs."

She turned back to her own room to get properly dressed, her mind already planning what she needed before she went to the car, how she would set up the GPS, whether she would have time to grab a flask of coffee to go.

***

Laura passed through the house, sidling past a deputy who was coming the other way with a pile of evidence markers in his hands, clearly packing away the ones they no longer needed. Agent Moore trailed behind her, still rubbing at sleepy eyes as they moved into the back yard—the source of the thrum of activity around the property.

"This is him?" Laura asked, which was unnecessary, but mostly used as a conversation starter.

"That's him," the Sheriff confirmed. "I know him. He's been a local here for his whole life—and he's got fifteen years on me. Hank Gregory. Widower. He lived here on his own since his wife passed."

"Children?" Laura asked.

"No, his son died a few years back as well," the Sheriff said. He made a tsk sound as he shook his head, looking down at the body a few yards away. "Poor guy. He had nothing left. At least there's no family left to mourn him."

"Do we know time of death?" Laura asked. "If he was on his own, might it have been days?"

"No, no." The Sheriff shook his head. "He has a nurse. Comes in every day to make sure he takes his medication, cleans up for him, that kind of thing. She usually makes him breakfast or lunch as well so he has at least one real meal a day. The rest of the time, he just about copes—not enough to put him in a home yet. No one to pay for it, even if he needed it. Anyway, she came over this morning, earlier than usual, and couldn't find him in the house. Looks like he might have been out there all night, according to Jerry."

Laura glanced up and saw the ME from the morgue, standing off to one side and jotting notes in a notebook. He nodded at her in greeting.

"Let's go take a look," Laura said, directing her comment to Agent Moore, who was skulking around behind her as if hiding from the early morning sunlight. "Then we'll need to speak to this nurse."

The Sheriff nodded. "I have her waiting inside, on Hank's sofa," he said. "She's had a shock. I'll sit with her until you're ready."

Laura nodded, then led Agent Moore over to the area of the yard that was staked out with crime scene tape, stopping anyone from getting too close. Jerry nodded to them again and then moved back

90

inside the house, having no doubt finished his initial observations. That left them alone with Hank—the victim.

He was an older man, and Laura's gut twisted in sympathy at his gray hair and lined hands. He'd never stood a chance, at his age.

Not that anyone would have, faced with the injuries he had. The attack had been brutal and sustained—the slashes across his body and throat attested to that. There was only one visible injury to his hands and arms, which made Laura believe he must have passed out or died before the rest of the wounds were inflicted—there would have been more defensive wounds if he was still fighting as the attack went on.

"God," Agent Moore gasped out, and Laura turned to see tears streaming down her cheeks. She was looking up at the horizon above the fence, as though she couldn't stand to look down.

Laura couldn't bring herself to say something critical. Not this time. The sight of the old man, rendered into something more fitting for the butcher's table than a residential street, would have been enough to reduce a lot of people to tears. And at least she hadn't thrown up this time.

There wasn't anything more the body could tell her until the medical examiner gave his report and the forensics tests came back. There was certainly nothing in the way of evidence lying around in the yard; no footprints, as far as Laura could see, in the closely mowed grass. It hadn't rained recently, and the ground was solid.

Whoever their killer was, he was good at covering his tracks.

She walked inside, allowing Agent Moore to follow her or not as she pleased—if she needed a moment, Laura would let her have it. But the rookie raced behind her, practically on her heels, and Laura had the impression that she didn't want to be left alone anywhere near the body.

"Alright," Laura said, stepping inside the living room with a sympathetic tone. She lifted her eyebrows at the Sheriff. "Nurse…"

"Joy White," he supplied.

"Ms. White, would you be able to answer a few questions for me? I know it's been a terrible shock."

"Yes," the nurse murmured, dabbing at eyes that seemed to already be dry with a crushed tissue held in her fist. She was sitting by the Sheriff on the sofa, dressed in a simple and unflattering uniform of blocky dark blue scrubs. She had personalized the outfit with a rainbow-colored shirt underneath, the long sleeves sticking out. Her dark hair was tied back tightly across the top of her head into a bun; she was younger than Laura, maybe closer to Agent Moore's age.

91

"Excellent," Laura said, sitting down quickly in a comfortable-looking armchair angled toward the television. It didn't disappoint. Agent Moore passed over to the other side of the room where a dresser held a collection of framed photographs, picking them up one by one to examine them. "Let's start with your discovery this morning."

"I came in early because Mr. Gregory was going out today," she said, sniffing. "He said he wanted to get everything done early."

"Where was he going?" Laura jumped in.

"He'd met some distant relatives," the nurse said. "He was having a barbecue with them today for his birthday. Oh, god—it was his birthday! Imagine getting killed on your birthday!"

"He was killed last night, if that helps," Agent Moore said, glancing over sympathetically.

Laura gritted her teeth. She would have preferred not to share information with the people connected to the case, just in case it would be important later. The suspect might incriminate themselves by knowing things like time of death if they were never told the details. It was too late now.

"These distant relatives," Laura said, sensing a connection here with a growing sense of unease. "When did he first meet them?"

"About a month ago," the nurse started. "There was this ancestors reunion thing, and—"

Laura was already unfolding the poster from her jacket pocket. "This one?"

"That's the one." The nurse nodded. "He was there. He'd been lonely the last few years."

Laura felt a rush in her blood. She'd assumed from the start that there was going to be a connection between this third victim and their first two—the same connection they had already identified. But to have it proven...

They were on the right track.

They might actually be able to do this.

"What about all these people?" Agent Moore asked. She was holding up one of the photographs from the dresser. There were so many of them. It looked as though Hank had had a vibrant family and social life—once.

"All dead," the nurse said, with a shrug of her shoulders that seemed to say *what can you do? That's life.*

Laura gave her a closer look; she didn't seem too upset, for all the Sheriff's talk of shock. She wasn't even sure the tissue in her hand had really been used. It seemed more like crocodile tears to her practiced eyes.

"This morning," she prompted. "You came in early…?"

"I couldn't find him anywhere, and then I noticed the back door from the kitchen was still open. I went out there and—and there he was. Oh, it's awful. I've been working with him for a year now!"

Aha. There it was. The nurse was upset that her client was gone, because that was what he'd been to her. A client. A way to earn a living. That was what Laura had been picking up in her odd vibe. She wasn't really sad about Hank at all.

Still, they needed to know about her alibi to rule her out. And there was valuable information coming through here, too: Hank had been lured outside. Whoever this was, they had struck three times in outdoor locations. They didn't want to, or maybe couldn't, break into the places they found their victims. That was good. Maybe if they sent out a county-wide warning to stay inside when on your own…

"Where were you yesterday?" Laura asked. "I'm interested in the whole day, through to when you came over this morning."

The nurse gave her a look of distaste, as if it was bad form to even ask her. "I was helping out Hank yesterday morning, then I went around my other patients—I've got a full day, every day. I clocked off work at seven and went home to my apartment, where I stayed all night long, asleep next to my boyfriend."

Laura nodded, jotting down a quick note to have someone check the alibi later. "And he was with you from the time you got home?"

"Yes, like normal." She nodded. "This isn't anything to do with me, you know. I've always looked after Hank. He liked me. I'm a good nurse."

"I'm sure you are," Laura said, not bothering to even try to make her voice sound truly reassuring. "Alright, thank you, Ms. White. If you think of anything, please let us know—and we'll be in touch if we have more questions."

The nurse nodded, but Laura was already ignoring her, trying to think about her next move.

The relationship between the three victims was very obviously genetic, and also tied to the reunion they had attended. But that was as far as they'd gotten.

Maybe it was time to jump down into the trenches and get dirty.

"What do we do now?" Agent Moore asked as they stepped outside.

"Now," Laura said grimly, wishing she didn't have to, "we interview our way through nearly two thousand people, one at a time, until we get some answers."

CHAPTER NINETEEN

Back at the Sheriff's station, Laura opened her emails to find a list of the most suspicious attendees of the reunion. There were a baker's dozen of them, all with criminal records or suspected involvement that hinted at a dark past. Suspicious enough to warrant following up.

But focusing on these few would mean ignoring all the others—and there were far too many of them to risk missing some pertinent information.

Laura spun the office chair around, facing Agent Moore. "Alright. This is how we're going to do it," she said. "I'm going to go out and talk to the people on this list. You're going to stay here."

"I don't get to come with you?" Agent Moore asked, pouting. She was like a child being told she couldn't have a treat. Laura resisted the urge to roll her eyes. The rookie was still young. If Laura was given the chance to sit back and take a backseat on a case, she'd jump at the chance to maybe relax just a tiny bit.

No, that was a lie. She'd insist on being hands-on anyway. With her ability, something that no one else could do, Laura had always felt like she was the only one to carry personal responsibility for each and every case she worked. The buck stopped with her, and she wasn't going to let a killer go unchecked.

"You're going to stay here because I have a task I need you to do in the meantime," Laura said, emphasizing the words heavily to let Agent Moore know that she had overreacted to the news. "You need to start calling your way through everyone else on this list. Get the basic questions answered: did they see anything suspicious or recall any kind of disturbance or argument? Did they know any of the victims or see them at the event? Have they noticed anything suspicious themselves at home? If you think they sound suspicious, get them to give you an alibi. Just bear in mind we don't have the manpower or resources to check out the alibis for all of them, so unless we have a good reason to suspect someone, their info will probably just need to sit on file."

"Right," Agent Moore said. "Um. How will I know if they're suspicious enough?"

Laura took a breath. "Okay, ask them all for alibis, but make a special note if you have reason to think they aren't telling the truth.

How's that? Oh, and make sure you do write down all of the information they give you."

"Got it," Agent Moore said. Then she did something unexpected: she beamed. "I'm going to talk to so many new people today!"

"Yes, you are," Laura agreed, with a sinking feeling that she tried hard to ignore. The rookie was going to be fine, right? She wasn't going to waste time with idle conversation and only manage to get through three calls by the time Laura was back... right? "Just keep it short and do as many as you can. We're going to be doing this until we get another lead, so the faster you get to the next name, the better."

"Got it, boss," Agent Moore said with a grin.

"You know," Laura started, intending to say that she wasn't Agent Moore's boss. Not really. They were partners. But then she got a look at the rookie's earnest face, and decided against it. No one needed her to get a sudden sense of autonomy. "I probably won't be back for lunch. So just go ahead without me."

"Sure!" Agent Moore called back, as Laura gathered her things and started to leave. "Just make sure you get something to eat, or you'll end up irritable and tired!"

Laura simply waved over her shoulder without looking back as she headed on to the first address the FBI techs had given her.

**

Seven interviews later, Laura got back into the hire car and sighed, shoving her hands back over her blonde hair and smoothing some of it back into the neat ponytail it had been this morning. What she really felt like doing was ripping the hair tie out and throwing it into the back of the car. Or possibly out the window. Anywhere, really, where she could throw it hard enough to sufficiently vent her frustration.

She just wasn't getting anywhere. So much driving around, running from one side of the county to the other, and she felt like she'd had a different story from every single person she'd spoken to. She grabbed her phone and called Agent Moore's number, waiting for it to connect.

"Hi, Agent Frost!" she enthused, sounding just as bright and bubbly as she had when Laura had left her this morning. "You just caught me between calls. That was lucky! Did you find something?"

"Not exactly," Laura sighed. "I'm getting a lot of conflicting opinions on how well the reunion went."

"What do you mean?" Agent Moore asked.

96

"Well," Laura said, rubbing a hand across her temple to try and ease some of the stress she felt. "Let's see. The first person I spoke to said that the reunion was the most exciting event they've ever been to in their lives, everyone had such a great time, it was a complete love fest, and she couldn't imagine anyone ever having any problem with one another since everyone was seemingly part of a big old perfect family they didn't even know about until that weekend. Oh, and she hasn't even been tempted to do any crimes since then, thanks to all the lovely goodwill that was spread around."

"Aww," Agent Moore started.

"But then," Laura continued, cutting off whatever she had been about to say, "the next person I spoke to said that it was the most boring thing he had ever been to and he wishes he'd never gone. He swore at me and called me some pretty misogynistic names when I tried to get an alibi from him and then yelled at me until I left his apartment, and then I had to call up his parole officer to find out he was actually at a parole check-in at the time of one of our murders anyway."

"Oh," Agent Moore replied. "Well. At least you didn't have to go back in with backup?"

"Yes, there is that." Laura shook her head in frustration. "But that was just the first two people. Every single one of them had a different version of events. Anyway. I thought I'd call because I actually did get something that might be useful from my last visit. I didn't really have anything useful until this one—some of them just made friends and enjoyed it, others thought it was dull and went home early. But this witness, who does have an alibi for the last two days, said that he witnessed someone making a big scene in front of a few dozen other people."

"A big scene?" Agent Moore paused. "I had a witness statement, actually…"

"Yes?" Laura prompted. "What did you hear?"

"One of my people from the list said that she saw someone yelling a lot and getting in someone's face," Agent Moore explained. "She didn't know what they were fighting about because she missed the start of the argument, but when she got closer she saw they were really going for it. She thought there was going to be physical violence, but then one of them walked away when his wife tugged on his arm and begged him to stop."

"That tallies pretty well with what I was just told," Laura said, sitting straighter. "In my witness's story, this man rushed over toward someone he already knew and demanded to know what he was doing there. When he said that he had been invited because he was related to the ancestors, and the first man realized that meant *they* were related, he lost it. The witness turned and rushed off to another part of the convention hall—he's been in trouble a lot but he's doing anger management classes now, and he didn't want to get caught up in something if it all kicked off."

"That's something, right?" Agent Moore asked. "And I did speak to the next person I called about it to see if they witnessed something. Well, the list is alphabetical, so it turns out that the next person was the brother of the woman I'd just spoken to. He saw the fight as well. He thinks he heard the first guy saying he was going to kill the second one."

"That's definitely something," Laura said. She was starting to feel some excitement. If there was something to this lead, then she was already starting to connect things and make assumptions in her head. There were two males involved, so perhaps the man who had been threatened was either James Bluton or Hank Gregory. And if they weren't involved in the fight directly, maybe this whole thing had stirred up an old rivalry between two groups who had reason to want one another harmed. There had been stranger disputes between neighbors, after all. "Do we have an ID on this angry, shouting man?"

"Yes," Agent Moore told her excitedly. "Both of my witnesses recognized the man who was shouting. He was one of their neighbors here, on a farmstead outside of town. They said he moved, though, so they don't know where he is now."

"There's one easy way to check," Laura said. "Do you have him on the attendance list?"

There was a long pause. Agent Moore was making a quiet noise, as though she was muttering to herself under her breath as she checked over the names. "Yes!" she exclaimed after a moment. "Yes, he's on here."

"And his address?"

"Yes!" Agent Moore said, sounding as though she'd just won the lottery. "It's right here in town!"

"Alright," Laura said. "Get yourself outside the station. I'll swing by and pick you up—I'm fifteen minutes away. Then we're going to talk to this man. What's his name?"

"Keegan Michaels."

"Michaels," Laura repeated. Just like their first victim.

This lead was getting more interesting by the minute.

CHAPTER TWENTY

Laura hopped out of the car almost before the engine had stopped, ready to get this case wrapped up and done with. She had a feeling it was going to take a bit more unraveling than could be done in a single interview, but she also liked the sound of her theory a lot.

A feud between two clans who found themselves actually related after all. One case of spilled blood leading to another in revenge. It didn't completely explain the matching MOs between each of the victims—but it could, if Keegan Michaels had seen Janae's body and knew how to mimic the same attack.

"Let me do all the talking," Laura warned Agent Moore, as they approached the front door of a small home sandwiched close between two others. The building looked like it had once been something bigger—a warehouse, possibly—that had been converted into small and affordable houses. "This is serious. If this is the one, we don't want to set him off in the wrong way. I'm good at getting people to talk, so let me try and lure him into a confession."

Agent Moore nodded. "I'll just try and stay quiet in the background," she said. There was something shining in her eyes, which made Laura very worried. "I can't wait to see you in action. I bet this is going to be a masterclass!"

"This isn't a classroom," Laura told her, keeping her voice quiet as they approached the door. "This is real life. With real consequences. Got it?"

"Sorry," Agent Moore whispered, cringing a little under the force of Laura's rebuke.

Laura squared her shoulders, pushed that all to the back of her mind, and knocked on the door.

In the few moments it took to hear movement inside the house, Laura noted a few things. First among them was that, while the neighbors kept their tiny front yards and facades neat and tidy, this lawn was in heavy need of weeding—and the paint was peeling on the door.

The second thing was the keyhole of the door itself, which was gouged with huge scratch marks all the way around the lock. Before she really had a chance to process the fact that she was certain she knew what that meant, the door was opening, and Laura had to be all business as she looked up at their suspect.

Who was dressed in a stained vest and sweatpants, looked as though he had been woken up by the door, and had large red blooms of broken blood vessels on his cheeks and nose that told Laura her first instinct had been right.

He was an alcoholic.

Laura cleared her throat, trying not to smell the alcohol that wafted from him. "Keegan Michaels?" she asked.

"Yeah," he said, nodding and then squinting at her. "Are you investigating Janae's death?"

Laura glanced surreptitiously at Agent Moore, internally begging her not to give the game away. "Yes," she said. "I'm sorry, can I just check—what was your relationship to her?"

"I'm her cousin," Keegan said, scratching his chest. He was probably in his thirties, though he had signs of aging that seemed as though they might be premature: wrinkles that were deeper on his forehead than anywhere else, faint gray hairs scattered throughout the untidy mess of brown strands on his head.

"Right." Laura nodded. "That's right. We're talking to her cousins, just to see if we can get any extra information to help us in the case. Can we come in?"

Keegan glanced up and down the street as if checking to see who was watching. "Fine," he said, after a moment, turning to lead them back into the dim interior of the house.

Laura took a deep breath, fearing it was going to be the last one she dared to take, and stepped inside.

The hallway was not immediately offensive. It was only when they followed Keegan into his living room that the smell arose. Stale alcohol, sweat, and rotten food. Laura had to clench her fists to stop herself from wanting to throw up or run out of the room.

There were several bottles sitting or lying on the table and the couch, and scattered across the floor. Some of them probably had a drop or two left in them. Laura clenched her fists so hard she felt her fingernails biting into her skin. She couldn't allow this to be temptation. She was here on a case. She had to be serious.

"Take a seat," Keegan said, dubiously gesturing to the single armchair with a broken side-rest and the couch, which he immediately flopped down onto, taking up all of the cushions.

He was a mess. Amongst the empty bottles were empty takeout boxes and plates still crusted with old food. The curtains were closed, and Laura could easily see that he had been sleeping on the couch—probably passing out in a drunken stupor and not bothering to get up again. There was far more than three days' worth of debris here. Whatever this was, it wasn't new. It hadn't been triggered by Janae's death.

"How have you been coping with your cousin's death?" Laura asked, a question that was supposed to be polite. An oblique way of getting at the real question she wanted to ask.

"This isn't because of Janae," Keegan said bluntly, waving a hand toward the mess. "I'm an alcoholic. Have been for a while. It's not because of her."

"Right," Laura said. At least that was taken care of. She glanced around again, but decided to remain standing. It was the best position to be in if she needed to run out of here. "Well. In that case, I'd like to ask you about your relationship with Janae, all the same. Were you close?"

Keegan shrugged and rubbed a hand over his face. "Used to be," he said. "When she was born, I was already a teenager. It was exciting, having a new baby cousin. I used to babysit for pocket money and stuff. Anyway, she grew up."

"I imagine that you were still very upset to learn that she had died," Laura said.

"Yeah," Keegan said, with another shrug. He looked tired. Bleary-eyed. The hand that passed over his face the second time was shaking. He needed a fix. She knew the signs well enough from having experienced them herself. "It was sad. It is sad. I guess I'm still processing it."

"It didn't make you angry?" Laura asked.

"What?"

Laura paused, changed tack. She didn't want him getting his back up too quickly. "Were you at the ancestors reunion that she attended last month? I gather you would have been invited, since you were related."

"Yes, I went," Keegan said, frowning slightly. "Made an ass out of myself, as usual."

He was making this far too easy for her. "How so?"

Keegan sighed, gestured around at the bottles as if that explained everything. "Got into a fight. Well, kind of. Screamed at him. What kind of loser lets themselves get into so much of a state, they become an alcoholic?" he asked, shaking his head miserably.

Laura said nothing, forcing a polite smile onto her face. In her pocket, she ran her fingers over the chip she always carried to remind her of how far she'd come.

She couldn't let his words, though they cut deep, derail this interview. He didn't even know he was talking to a fellow alcoholic. He was talking about himself, not about her.

"Can you tell me exactly what happened, and why?" Laura asked. "This could be very important to our investigation."

He cast a sideways look at her. "I doubt that."

"Let me be the judge," Laura insisted.

Keegan sighed and took a breath. Laura recognized in him an emotion she'd borne herself: the knowledge that you had to tell a story of the shameful thing you had done when drunk. "I used to have a wife, before all this. Or maybe it wasn't before. I don't know. It's kind of hard to tell when the drinking became a problem and whether it was before or after she left."

"She left you?" Laura asked. She wanted clarification to be sure that it was a case of a marriage breaking up, and not a death.

"Yeah, she decided to shack up with this guy from work that she'd been sleeping with," Keegan said, his shoulders slumping even further at the memory. "Turns out they'd been doing it for months. So, they ended up living together, and I was on my own, so I couldn't afford the house anymore. I ended up having to move here because it was the only place I could afford that was on the market and close enough to work. Which I ended up getting fired from, anyway, so here we are."

Laura nodded impatiently. "So, getting back to what happened at the reunion?"

"Right." Keegan's hand twitched toward one of the bottles on the table as if he wanted to check whether there was anything in it, but then he looked away. It looked empty anyway. "I thought the reunion might be a chance to get a bit of a fresh start, you know? Maybe meet some relatives I didn't know I had, cheer me up about being on my own these days. Only, I walk around the corner, and who do I see? My wife and her new man, just standing there arm in arm like butter wouldn't melt."

Agent Moore let out a low whistle. Laura and Keegan both swiveled to look at her; she had been so quiet until then that Laura had actually forgotten she was in the room. She looked guilty at the interruption, shrinking under both of their gazes.

"I couldn't help myself." Keegan shrugged. "I'd already had a few drinks to give me some courage before I went to the convention hall, you know? I didn't have it in me to hold back. I went for him. Started yelling about how he stole my woman, and she was just standing there all embarrassed, giving me that look like she used to when I did something to show her up in public."

Laura couldn't help but wince. She felt like she could relate. After all, she'd done plenty to make an idiot out of herself back when things were really bad. Even Nate had looked at her like that once. And she'd like to say that that had been the catalyst that made her stop drinking—but it hadn't been. Not by a long shot.

"What was said?" Laura asked. She wanted him to tell her, himself, about the threats.

"I threatened to kill him," Keegan said, then burst out into self-pitying laughter. "Can you imagine? I can barely walk around, the shakes are so bad if I don't drink. And when I do drink, I can barely walk in a straight line anyway. Me, trying to kill someone? I'd probably just end up hurting myself."

He was doing a pretty good job of making himself seem innocent, even though he was also doing a pretty good job of confessing everything. He had a good point about his abilities—but that wasn't enough to rule him out fully, not to be absolutely certain about it.

"Mr. Michaels," Laura said. "Can I ask you where you've been for the past three days?"

"Here." Keegan shrugged, the answer coming easily. "I don't go out much anymore. I've just been sitting here."

"On your own?"

He nodded confirmation.

Not much of an alibi.

"Do you have anything that would prove you were here?" Laura asked.

"Nope," Keegan said. He seemed completely unfazed by the fact that he was clearly being asked for an alibi and had nothing to give. Perhaps because of what he'd said earlier—he was so confident that anyone would be able to see there was no chance he'd be able to really do any harm. "Oh, there might be. I ordered some takeout this week on my app. I always get the same driver. I don't tip him, so he probably remembers me pretty well."

"You don't tip him?" Agent Moore gasped, interjecting once again despite her promise that she wouldn't. "That's really bad!"

Keegan nodded. "I know," he said. "But he's bringing me my drinks. And if I tip him, I won't be able to buy as many. You see?"

103

"Alright," Laura said, wanting to stop this part of the conversation in its tracks before they got off on a tangent that nobody needed. "So, this guy who stole your wife. What's his name?"

"John something. I don't know. I just stalk their Instagram posts. They went out for a nice romantic meal last night. Made me want to get unconscious—which I did."

"Bluton? Gregory?"

Keegan blinked. "No, I don't think so."

Laura sighed. She wasn't annoyed with Keegan Michaels, exactly, but she was starting to think that he wasn't related to their case at all. Her whole theory meant nothing if the other man wasn't connected to at least one of the other victims. And since the other man and Keegan's ex-wife hadn't come to any harm since the event, it was more and more obvious that she'd been wrong.

"Alright," Laura said. She turned her body back toward the door. "I think that's everything we need to know for now. We'll be in touch if there's more."

"Wait," Keegan said. "Janae's killer. Do you know who it is yet? I mean, you have any ideas?"

"We're not able to comment on any leads we might be following until the investigation is complete," Laura said quickly, wanting to cut off any chance of Agent Moore blurting out an answer.

"So, you have leads," Keegan said, brightening a little. "That's great. At least you'll be able to stop him, make sure Janae gets some justice. She was a great girl, you know?"

"I'm sure," Laura said, with a polite, tight smile, and walked out of Keegan Michaels's home and back to the car.

Inside, a voice in her head was taunting her with the truth of it all: *you don't have a single useful lead or any idea where to go next.*

Which meant the chances of Janae's killer getting away with it were rising by the hour—and so was the chance of him being able to strike again.

CHAPTER TWENTY ONE

He walked in the shadows where he could, but during the day, it was more difficult to hide. Especially out on these rural roads, where you had to have an excuse for being on them in the first place. A car would be an obvious sore thumb, sticking out in all the wrong ways, blowing his cover.

He'd thought of that, though. He'd figured it out a while back, when he'd first started this whole thing. He first drove to a field that was popular with walkers of some kind. Dog walkers. Fishermen going to a local river. Birdwatchers, even. That needed a little research and thought, but it wasn't as though he wasn't familiar with the local area. He could find the kind of place that would work easily enough.

Then he would park and get out. That was important. He had to bide his time to make sure no one else was around, and also wear a disguise—something that would make him blend in for plausible deniability. He carried a walking stick when he went to locations that were popular with ramblers. At the fishing locations, he wore waders and a waterproof coat. Always, he tried to wear the colors of the scenery: greens, dark and light, gold for the corn, never anything bright or out of place.

Then he walked. It was simple as that: he walked to the place he needed to see. This one was a challenging one. He had to walk pretty far. But it was fine, because it was a dog walking spot he'd parked at, and all he had to do was pretend his dog had run off and get the old chewed-up tennis ball from his pocket that he'd taken from a neighbor's yard.

That was enough for him to sneak right up near the house and watch, and wait for her to come home from work. He'd done it yesterday, between his other commitments, and a few times over the last weeks as well—whenever he had the chance. He'd marked off every day of the week, and she was always home at the same time, except on the weekends.

It was a reliable schedule. He just had to wait and watch for her to go off for her shift this morning, to be sure that there was no unexpected change, and then the plan would be set.

He settled in to wait and watch.

You're going to get her, aren't you?

It was *her*. She was here. "Yes," he said out loud, not needing to think about his answer. "Yes, of course I will. You told me to."

You're willing to make sure she pays, as they all need to?

"Yes. Yes, I told you. I promised."

In my experience, men do not always keep their promises.

He sighed. "I know. But you can trust me, I swear. Haven't I done good for you so far?"

Her thought was like the warm weight of a purring cat along him, a satisfied rumble through his mind and body. *Yes. You've done everything I asked of you so far.*

"Right. And I'll carry on. I don't want to let you down."

You won't if you just follow as I've asked, she said, and he felt her words making him stand taller, feel stronger. *You're so far in now, and so close to the end. All you have to do is to keep going, just as you are. Just keep going strong. End them all. End the bloodline before any more come. Don't let them multiply.*

"I won't," he said. "I mean it. I'll make sure there can't be any more. I will do this for you—right to the very end."

Right to the end, she whispered, almost as if she were standing right next to him. *You'll be rewarded. You know you will. I will keep my end of the bargain once you have kept yours.*

"I believe you," he said, because he did, and he knew she could feel the truth in it. He knew by how she settled, like a weight on his shoulders, like she was leaning lovingly on him from behind.

He stopped talking then, and she did too, their attention taken by something else. The woman. She was coming out of her house, walking down the driveway to her car. He checked his watch. She was right on time.

Everything was set for tonight—and he wasn't going to miss the chance to get her when she came home.

CHAPTER TWENTY TWO

Laura drove the short distance back to the Sheriff's station chewing her lip, unable to think of a single thing to do next other than what they had already been doing. She only stopped when she tasted blood, realizing she had bitten right through the delicate skin under the force of her own thoughts.

"Are we just going to keep on calling people?" Agent Moore asked. She sounded dejected. Like she'd been counting on the lead to pan out.

She wasn't the only one.

"Yeah," she said, parking in front of the station and resting for a moment, her hands still on the steering wheel. "Yeah, you head in and keep going through your list. Let me know if something comes up."

Agent Moore nodded at her with a bright smile, apparently finding the energy from somewhere to raise herself up. "It'll work out, you'll see," she said. "I'm sure you'll think of something. Or there'll be a lead from the rest of the calls. You're Special Agent Laura Frost—I've heard enough about your cases to know you're going to solve this one, just like all of the others."

Agent Moore opened her door and got out of the car, practically skipping into the station. Apparently, it wasn't possible to keep her down for long.

Laura sighed, rubbing a hand across her face now that she was alone. The "superhero agent who knows how to solve every single case" thing was already wearing thin. It was a lot of pressure. She wanted to solve the case, obviously, but at least if Agent Moore had a little less faith in her she might end up trying harder.

What was she going to do now?

Sit there and call every single person on the list, along with Agent Moore, until they ran out of names and still didn't have any leads? This was a needle in a haystack situation. Except the haystack was also full of needles. They knew it had to be someone from that bloodline who was at that convention, but—

But, did they?

No, Laura realized, sinking her head into her hands even more. They didn't even know that. They were aware of the connection between the victims, but that was all. And if they didn't work on this fast, they would be looking at the body of a fourth victim tomorrow morning.

She knew what she needed. *Who* she needed. She just…

Didn't know whether it was alright for her to need him anymore.

But lives were at risk, and Laura was tired, and she needed help. Her hands did it almost without consulting her brain—picking up her cell phone, finding Nate's number, pressing call. And then she was waiting, the phone pressed to her ear, the incessant dial tone an unwelcome companion for the delay.

And then it hit his voicemail message, and Laura hung up quicker than she'd moved in a long time. The last thing she wanted was to record an awkward message—even a few seconds of silence.

He hadn't picked up. He was still ignoring her.

She took a breath, but it stung in her chest. She found herself double-gasping, a sob wracking her body which she hadn't expected. She wiped her eyes quickly, stared out of the window across an empty plain toward the fields, braced her fist against her mouth. She needed to keep it together.

But this was shaping up to be one of the hardest cases to get started on that she'd ever come across, for one reason or another, and she just didn't know when the rainclouds were going to part and show her the way illuminated before her.

There wasn't any time for wallowing.

Laura forced herself to open the car door and get out, following in Agent Moore's footsteps. She found her right where she expected her to be: sitting at the same table in the small bullpen, calling her way through the list. She was just putting the phone down as Laura walked in, and she beamed at her.

"You got something?" Laura asked, seizing onto that look immediately.

"Not yet!" Agent Moore exclaimed. "But I just got to cross another name off the list, so we're that much closer to finding out who did it!"

That much closer. Maybe that was the way she should be thinking about it.

Every step forward they took was a step in the right direction. So what if the steps were taking longer than they usually did? They were still moving forward. The killer couldn't outrun them forever. Sooner or later they would find him, or he would make a mistake. Hell, maybe he already had. They were still waiting for Jerry's report on the most recent body, after all.

She was going to get this one. She had to.

"I'm going to head next door, talk to Jerry," she said. "Oh—what's this?" She had almost tripped over a filing box that was sitting on the floor by the desk, right where she wanted to turn to walk out of the room again.

"That's evidence from the case," the old-timer deputy, who was still sitting in his spot at the back of the room, spoke up. "The Sheriff left it there earlier. He asked where you were sitting and I said there. Then he went right back out again. Guess it's a busy one this week, huh?"

"Well, there is a serial killer on the loose," Laura said, tilting her head and considering her words as she stooped to pick up the box. "Or a spree killer. Time will tell."

She put the box up on the desk and took off the lid, starting to rifle through the contents. Most things were sealed in bags or tubes, but she flipped through each one to examine it. There was junk mail that had apparently been waiting on Hank Gregory's doormat in the morning. Bracelets that Janae Michaels had been wearing when she died, but which had not been found to have any forensic value. Even a sample of the corn from the field where James Bluton had been found.

Laura picked up the next evidence bag, holding a bloodied handkerchief that had been in Hank Gregory's pocket, thinking to herself that she was getting tired because her head was starting to hurt just a little again, and—

She was there again, in the field. In that time so many years ago. Generations.

They were talking, just like before. They were standing around, the three of them, gesturing loosely to the field, one of them leaning on some kind of stick. A walking stick, maybe, or for hitting the corn to create a path, or Laura didn't know what else. She wasn't a farming expert.

Then, as before, the one who was facing back over the rise of the hill, looking up beyond where the house was in modern times, looked up and his face dropped. He screamed. He turned and began to run away, and within a few moments, the others did the same and followed. Laura saw their faces as they noticed whatever it was that was behind them.

There was a clear hierarchy as they ran. She turned to follow them, almost as if she was fleeing in their footsteps.

Or chasing them.

The one who had seen the threat first led the way, far out in front, clearly the least at risk of whatever it was that they were running from.

109

Then there was another man, and the last, the one who had carried the stick, was at the back. He was slower than his companions, so much so that he seemed to be falling behind with every step. He was desperate, but not enough.

There was a flash of silver in front of her—a curved blade slicing across his back. A blade on a long handle. Blood flew across her vision, thrown up into the air by the arc of the blade, splattered high and wide. She felt more than heard the screams turn to cries of agony as the man who had been last fell to the ground, his back carved open, blood pouring from it in huge gushes.

He was dying—that much was clear. The slash was so deep that Laura saw a white flash of bone. Blood was pouring out at a rate so fast he surely couldn't survive long. But the scythe came down again all the same, viciously tearing at him as he begged for his life, turning to look over his shoulder, his eyes wide and staring—

Laura caught the evidence bag she almost dropped, then placed it back into the box carefully.

She was processing what she had seen, and it was giving her new hope. She was on the right track, wasn't she? The victims in her vision were killed with great slashes of a large blade—just the same as the victims they were dealing with today.

It left her with many questions still to answer. Chief among them was the fact that time travel did not exist, so how was it that she was seeing a vision from long ago in the past that seemed to warn of the same killer she was dealing with now?

But she did have one gain from the vision that she could work on right away. An idea that had formed as she watched it happen, knowing that it was the mirror image of what was happening here. No, make that two things: first, that the murder weapon was a scythe, something used for farm work—and probably not as regularly these days, either.

Second, that she knew where she needed to go next.

"I've changed my mind about Jerry," she announced to Agent Moore. She nodded at her list of names on the desk. "Bring your phone and your list. You can continue making calls on the drive over. Come on—let's go."

CHAPTER TWENTY THREE

Laura was still wrestling with the concept of how to cover up the fact she'd had a vision as they approached the dilapidated office building again. She couldn't exactly walk in there and say that she'd had a vision of the past which connected an identical historic crime with what was happening here. She needed an excuse—a way to explain how the idea had come to her.

She couldn't just say that she'd driven there on a whim. Could she?

It was a long way to come just for that. Surely if it was only a whim, she would have done some research first. Looked it up herself or at least called ahead before visiting in person. It had to be more than just a whim.

Unless, of course, she just pretended that she *had* done some research.

"Why are we here again?" Agent Moore asked, puzzled, as she came up behind Laura. She was delayed, having still been on the phone to one of the reunion attendees when they pulled up. Apparently, she was now done with that particular conversation.

"To chase down another lead," Laura said. "Who better to tell us about something connected to the family bloodline than someone who has already researched it extensively? Anyway, I take it you don't have any new leads."

"Nope," Agent Moore said cheerfully. "I've managed to get through nearly a hundred people, though!"

For a moment, Laura actually felt impressed. Then she remembered that there were almost two thousand people to get through, and the feeling faded.

Maybe she should have instructed that old deputy to start calling people—but it looked as though the Sheriff only trusted him to sit at his desk and take on any calls that came through in an absolute emergency when everyone else was busy, rather than deploying him as a go-to. He probably wasn't very reliable. Laura wasn't sure exactly what kind of work he was even doing at that desk.

"Let's head up," Laura said, gesturing toward the building in front of them. She tried the door, having developed a suspicion last time they were here; it opened. In spite of the buzzer system, it seemed that there was no need to call ahead, since the door lock didn't work properly in the first place.

She walked up the now-familiar route to the genealogist's office, stopping and knocking on it rather than just bursting in. She could hear the low murmur of a voice coming from inside. It stopped abruptly when she knocked; then she heard a few more quick words before the sound of someone's rapid steps across the floor.

"Hello? Oh," Alice Papadopoli said, looking up and recognizing both Laura and Agent Moore. "Well, you'd better come in."

"Thank you," Laura said, stepping into the office after her. The small space felt cozier today. Maybe it was because she was no longer shocked by the state of the building itself and how it seemed to foreshadow a much less professional business. Perhaps it was that the weather had dropped colder out there, leaving the small heated office to feel like an island of warmth. Whatever it was, she almost welcomed stepping inside today.

"I take it this is in regards to the murders again?" Alice said, giving a little shudder as she sat back down behind her desk. She had a thin shawl-like garment over her shoulders today—Laura recognized that it was probably some kind of fashionable scarf that she had picked up in the eighties, but she couldn't help associating it with the old-fashioned farmers she had seen in her vision.

"It is," Laura confirmed, taking one of the chairs in front of the desk. "I had a bit of a thought, and I did a little research to follow up on it. I think you'll probably be best placed to tell us more about what I found."

"Go on," Alice said, sounding very intrigued. She even leaned forward a little in her chair.

Laura didn't look at Agent Moore as she explained; she didn't want to give herself away. She just hoped the younger rookie didn't figure out that Laura hadn't had enough time to do this kind of research—or that if she had done it much earlier, she hadn't mentioned it to her partner at all. "I found there was a vicious attack back in the earlier days of the farming community here," she said, picking her phrasing carefully to sound specific while actually being as vague as possible. She didn't really have the details, but she needed Alice to hear what she said and know what she was talking about. "A scythe was used as the weapon. Did you come across that while looking into your ancestry?"

"Ah." Alice nodded, drawing the shawl tighter about her as if she felt a sudden chill. "Yes, the massacre of 1825. Of course, it was a huge event in our state's history. Although I'm not sure what that can possibly have to do with your case today."

"You've heard of copycat killers, yes?" Laura said. She hadn't quite figured out the connection herself, yet, but this was the obvious explanation. It might even be the right one. She needed more information to know whether that really was the case or not.

"I see." Alice nodded. "Then I suppose you want to know everything you can about it." She stood up, moving just a couple of steps to the back of the room where a large, dark wood bookcase stood filled with leather-bound books. Some of them looked historical, with faded and cracked spines, while others were more modern imitations. The one that Alice took down was a curiously new-looking volume, though the paper was heavy and yellow as if it had been printed in a bygone time.

"What's that?" Agent Moore gaped. "It's huge! I'm surprised you can lift it."

Alice chuckled, smoothing down the first page as she laid it open. "It is indeed very heavy," she said. "But that's because it is very important. For me, anyway. This is the results of my work on investigating my own family tree. I had it printed up professionally, so this is the only copy. I'll ask you to be careful with it, though I already know you will be."

Laura cast a warning look at Agent Moore to not even touch the thing. If she did, they would probably end up in some terrible romantic comedy movie sequence of spilled coffees, stumbles that resulted in torn pages, and something involving the very small window on one side of the room.

"You traced back your family tree through all the branches you could find? How far back?" Laura asked, seeing the neat diagrams printed on each page. The first page had just held a single family unit: Alice and, obviously from the line that connected them, her parents. From then, each page held a new branch spiking off into the past.

"As far as I could," Alice explained. "Some of the branches go back into the 1700s and I even managed to find one Dutch relative from the 1600s, although the records are so patchy that I couldn't identify who their wife was or anything about their parentage. That's where it all ends. Still, I'm pretty pleased with how far back I managed to go. Every time I found a new branch, I spent time tracing that down to present day as well, so I had as much complete information as possible. You'll find most of the attendees from the reunion here, too."

"The deceased?" Laura asked.

Alice flipped back through a few pages; she obviously knew the spiderweb-like trees well enough to be able to estimate whereabouts each one could be found in the book. "Here," she said, tapping one branch. Janae Michaels was right at the end, underneath her parents' names, with no siblings. Another page showed the same story for James Bluton, with a line for marriage connecting him to Maria. The line of parentage extended from her to her two children, but not from James, who of course was not their biological father. The third page, belonging to Hank Gregory, bore the names of both his wife and his son, both of them marked with a (d.) for deceased.

"You'll need to update this," Laura noted. She felt a tinge of sadness at it. It was always tragic to see loss of life, of course, but she was also used to it. Something like this, this official document which recorded the victims as being alive, seemed to drive it home in a totally different way. There was also the fact that this book had clearly been a labor of love on Herculean proportions, and to see it reduced to being inaccurate so quickly was a real shame.

"It's an historical document now," Alice noted, with a certain amount of philosophy. "A record of what the family tree looked like at that point in time. Anyway, this is what I wanted to show you." She flipped back many more pages to a place near the end of the records, to a branch of a tree that appeared to begin with relatives born in 1770 and later. There were a large number of entries spreading across the page, but each of them seemed to be the end of the line: even where the last member of the branch was married, there was nothing after them. No children. A whole branch of the tree that had simply ended with no progeny.

"What happened here?" Laura asked, even though she was starting to put the pieces together herself. A whole branch with no more leaves. Everyone dead. The death dates—she could see they were all the same.

A massacre.

Everyone killed at once.

"It was a shocking time," Alice said, shaking her head. "There was a terrible year. First, the crops were going black in some parts of the county, but not others. Of course, back at that time, this was just a small collection of farms loosely grouped around a few general stores, built in timber with names like 'bank' and 'dry goods' painted above the doors. But there was a rash of ergot. It spread across all of the fields but one. There, the corn stayed healthy. Of course, they didn't know about ergot back then—they just knew there wasn't much they could

114

salvage, so what they could salvage, they ate. They didn't have anything else."

Laura frowned. "Why was one field unaffected?"

Alice reached behind herself and pulled a large sheet of paper from a nearby shelf—as she placed it on the desk, it turned out to be a map of the surrounding area. "This is the location of the field," she said, tapping it with one finger. "See how the land lies? It's in a natural valley, and it also has the river right beside it. It's almost a closed ecosystem because of the shape of the land. Now, ergot is spread by wind, by physical contact, by insects, and by rainwater. The wind for the most part blows above the valley, leaving the ground underneath protected. The insects stuck to the banks of the river rather than going out of the valley, for the most part. Rainwater follows the path of least resistance and the shape of the valley encourages it to fall to either side—it would be dry down here if it wasn't for the river flowing across. And as for physical contact, people kept to themselves. They wouldn't be wandering across one another's land. That would lead to conflict—you might get shot at if people assumed you were a native raider or a stranger come from out of town."

"But they didn't know that at the time."

"I bet they thought it was witches," Agent Moore gasped. For once, Laura didn't feel the urge to scowl at her. Her childish enthusiasm was a little misplaced, but otherwise, Laura couldn't see that she was wrong.

"There was a lot of suspicion at that time," Alice confirmed. "Now, the fields at the time were mostly owned by a few members of the same family. Cousins, brothers, and sisters with their spouses and children. A man died earlier in the year, before the harvest began. He was one of the elders of the family, whose idea it had been to come to the new world in the first place. He'd been responsible for the initial land purchase and for dividing up the farming fields between the different farmers. Once he was dead, and the crops were only prospering in one spot, the remaining family members started to dispute whether he had really meant for those divisions to be the way they were at all."

"It was a perfect storm," Laura said. "Madness from the ergot, the desperation of hunger, the feud…"

"That's why one of the men turned on the rest of the family," Alice said. "He started with his uncle, who owned the fields here that never caught ergot. Two of his cousins were there and he slaughtered them too. From there, he just continued on. It was like he had a madness for

115

blood and couldn't be stopped. By the time the day was over, he had wiped out almost all of his own extended family."

"Almost?" Laura asked. She knew an important detail when she heard one. She wasn't going to let that slip out of her hands.

Alice turned the page. There was another tree there, a branch that shot sideways from the edge of the page. "This is the killer's list of descendants. He did not kill his own wife or children." She turned the page again, twice, to flip to the other side of the wiped-out tree. "Here, I have all of the descendants of the lone survivor. A woman. She was due to marry another local farmer and had been visiting the church with his family, chaperoned by the groom's mother."

Laura stared at the book for a long moment, trying to organize her thoughts and process what she was seeing. "You're telling me that, nearly two hundred years ago, a whole family died except for two distantly related members—in the exact same way that people are dying now—and there are modern descendants of both the killer and the victims who are alive now?"

"The exact same way?" Alice repeated sharply. "Do you mean to say that the victims were killed with a scythe, mown down in the fields?"

In the fields, Laura thought. Only there weren't as many fields out there now as there used to be. No, the killer had had to improvise—to go for the next best thing.

He'd had to settle for backyards.

"This is our link," she said. "The massacre. Somehow, it's linked to what's happening today. Now we just have to figure out how."

CHAPTER TWENTY FOUR

"Show me the pages of our victims again," Laura said. "Let's start with the first one—Janae Michaels."

Alice nodded and flipped back through the pages, muttering to herself quietly until she found it again. "Here."

"Right." Laura nodded. She looked up at the top of the page. There was a notation next to the male family member who had fathered the children to start off this particular part of the tree: *see page 82.* "Now to page eighty-two."

This page had a notation at the top to turn to page 113. Laura nodded for her to do it, and—

"There!" Laura stopped her, excited now, tapping the page they had turned to. It was familiar enough. There, right in the middle of the page, was the man who had done it all. The killer.

And the line of descendancy went right from him through the next two pages and down to Janae Michaels.

"Now James Bluton," Laura said. She thought she already knew what they were going to see, but she needed to have it confirmed. She needed to be sure.

Alice traced it back over the page, and then—"Turn to page one hundred thirteen," she read aloud, looking up at Laura.

Laura nodded grimly. "What about this line?" she asked. "It goes up from Maria—but she shouldn't be on the chart connected to anyone else, should she?"

Alice made a face. "Eight generations in one small area is a long time. You might be surprised." She followed the notation to turn to page 128 from Maria's name, the line having nowhere else to go without intersecting with James's family's line, and then nodded. "Yes, here we are. She was a distant cousin of her husband's. So very distantly that it hardly mattered at all, however."

Laura chewed this information over.

"And Hank Gregory?"

He was an older man, and his position in the tree was higher than the other two. But the trace through his forefathers led them to the same spot.

Page 113.

"Ebediah Michaels," Laura said. "Our massacre killer was the ancestor of all three of our new victims. This is it. This is the link." She slapped her hand on the side of the table victoriously, looking around to grin at Alice and Agent Moore—both of whom seemed to share her enthusiasm.

They'd done it.

They'd found their link, and it was a link that explained everything. A massacre that happened two centuries ago might not seem recent enough to warrant deaths today, but there were generational feuds that had lasted for as long. Families who had long lived and interbred in a certain part of the country, whose opponents had done the same. This being technically all part of the same family was another issue, but it was clear that more branches had survived than the one that was wiped out.

Even in the same moment of elation at the fact that she had worked it out, Laura felt her heart drop again.

"But aren't there thousands of people alive today from the same bloodline?" Agent Moore said, speaking Laura's disappointment out loud. "More even than went to the reunion! How are we supposed to know who could be a target, or who the killer is?"

"We can't," Laura said, crestfallen. She pressed her fingertips against her temple, trying to think. "Any one of the people who are descended from the same family could be at risk. So far, we only have victims who were both descended exactly from Ebediah Michaels and at the reunion, but that doesn't necessarily mean only people in those categories are at risk here. Even if they were... how many are left alive?"

Alice flipped the pages quickly. From Ebediah Michaels and his wife, an uncomfortably large number of progeny shot down the page, their lines connecting to more children and more. Alice worked fast, counting. "Sixteen," she said. "There are twenty-one living descendants of Ebediah Michaels. No, wait—twenty-two. I forgot to count a grandfather, there."

"Definitely still alive?" Laura asked.

"When I went to print, which was just before the convention last month." Alice nodded. "I haven't heard on the grapevine of any deaths other than the three we know about."

Laura rubbed a hand over her mouth, considering it. "Twenty-two. It's too many. Even considering that many of them will be in the same households..."

"Eight family groups," Alice supplied helpfully.

"Even then," Laura continued, "we've got, what? Two deputies who are so busy we haven't even seen them, the Sheriff, the other deputy who seems a little past his best, and us. Six people. We could try to draft in reinforcements from nearby areas, but even if we do—to offer the best protection there should really be two officers at each site, and the two of us should be focusing on investigating, not sitting out front of a house all night long…"

"We don't have the manpower," Agent Moore sighed. "You know, Ms. Papadopoli, it's not like what you see on the TV at all. There's no budget for anything and you have to do it all yourself."

Alice nodded sagely, which seemed to brighten Agent Moore's day.

"We can't protect all the people we need to protect," Laura said grimly. "We can warn them, if we can get hold of them. The best course of action would be to figure out where the killer is going to strike next and intercept him, stop him from attacking. But I don't know how he's choosing who to go after. It might just be based on who is easiest to get to, in which case he'll just attack whoever we don't manage to protect."

"Well," Agent Moore said, but hesitantly, as if she wasn't sure whether she was about to get told off for speaking up. "Instead of protecting the potential victims, what if…"

"Go on," Laura prompted, when she didn't finish the sentence.

Agent Moore blushed and fidgeted. "It might be nothing. But what if we try to find the killer instead?"

"I would love to find the killer," Laura said, spreading her hands open in front of herself. "I just don't have enough leads to go on. That's why I'm suggesting protecting the victims. If I could figure out who the killer is, he would already be in handcuffs."

"Right," Agent Moore said, shaking her head and looking down as though she felt stupid. "It's just… we could maybe look into the descendants of the sole survivor?"

Laura blinked.

The sole female survivor—yes! She went on to have a family of her own, but she would have been deeply scarred by what had happened to her parents, siblings, aunts and uncles, and cousins. That kind of thing could be passed down in legend through a family, from parent to child and to their children after. Or if someone discovered they were related to this killer and blamed them for… what? A perceived lack of wealth or opportunity which might have been granted if their ancestors were allowed to farm in peace?

119

"That could work," she said. "Ms. Papadopoli? Do you know who would fit that bill?"

Alice eagerly flipped through her book, back to the page that mapped the tree of their sole survivor. "You know, when I made this book, I was worried it was a vanity project that I would end up never looking at again," she said, with a slight smile on her face. A look of pride and enjoyment in the tools she was using, rather than glee that someone had had to die for it to happen. "Here we are. Right, there have been seven generations since her. Looks like there are six descendants still alive."

"That's a much smaller number to work with," Laura said. "Their ages? How many are elderly?"

Alice consulted her figures. "Just one," she said. "A man in his seventies."

"We can rule him out," Laura said. "Anything you can tell us about the others?"

Alice nodded quickly, skimming her finger along the page to read the names again. "Three of them are aged between forty and fifty years old," she said. "Then we have two children of those adults, who are both adults now themselves. There were a couple more, actually, but there have been some deaths prior to all of this happening. If I remember from my research, it was… one car crash, and… yes, I think she was the poor child who died of leukemia."

"The living members—anything about them?" Laura asked. "Any of them have a dark past, history of mental illness, anything you've heard on the grapevine or while doing your research…?"

Alice hummed low, looking troubled. "I don't know if I should say it," she said. "I don't like to get someone in trouble if it turns out they aren't connected to all of this at all."

"You won't get them in trouble," Laura said. "You're just helping us join the dots quicker. We'll find out who is doing all of this eventually—let's do it now, before anyone else has to die."

That seemed to help Alice make up her mind. "Alright." she nodded. "There was a man—one of the older generation, I think he's in his mid-forties now. He doesn't have children of his own. Allan McLean. I don't really know too much about him, because we've never met."

"He didn't attend the reunion?" Agent Moore asked, sounding flabbergasted that anyone would choose to do such a thing.

"He wasn't invited," Alice said, making a guilty expression. "You see, the thing is, I didn't want to make trouble by inviting someone who had a criminal record."

That got Laura sitting bolt upright in her chair. "What kind of record?"

"Um," Alice said, tapping her fingers against her mouth fretfully. "Well, you see, I believe it was... some kind of violent act that got him some time in prison."

Laura almost exploded out of her chair. That sounded like a likely lead if ever she'd heard one. "Alice, I'm going to need you to give me all the information you collected on this man. Including his address, if you managed to find that at all. Agent Moore, head back to the car now—on the way, make a call to the Sheriff. We need him and his deputies making calls to all twenty-two of the at-risk victims. When you've done that, ask the Sheriff to look up Allan McLean and his record. Got it?"

"Yes, ma'am," Agent Moore replied, jumping up and rushing out into the hall as Alice turned to start printing pages of information from her computer.

They had him. And this time, Laura wasn't going to give him the chance to get away and target someone else.

CHAPTER TWENTY FIVE

Laura hit the brakes hard, sending Agent Moore almost flying through the windshield if it wasn't for her seatbelt. "Sorry," she threw out, but the word was probably lost on the wind; both of them already had their doors open and belts off before the engine had even stopped purring, running toward the door of the building ahead of them as fast as they could.

Agent Moore arrived first, having the advantage of stepping out of the passenger side of the car. She hammered on the door immediately, making a surprisingly loud noise for such a petite and naïve-looking woman. "Open up!" she shouted. "FBI!"

Laura joined her on the step, feeling the adrenaline shooting through her. Her senses were on high alert. There didn't appear to be any backyards in this street, with the houses shoved in close together, small and cramped and run-down. Still, she didn't discard the possibility of him trying to run, maybe climbing out of a window at the back of the house. She was straining her ears for any sign of movement, trying to catch shadows moving through the windows, anything to tell her what to expect next.

There was nothing. Only an eerie silence that left her feeling more convinced than ever they were on the right track. Something about that empty house, lonely and falling apart, seemed like a good metaphor for the kind of person who would lose their mind and carry out a rampage like this.

"FBI! Open up or we're coming in!" Agent Moore yelled. Laura found herself blinking. There was a surprising amount of ferocity coming out of the rookie, her auburn ponytail flashing from side to side with the strength of her heavy knocks. She looked stern, all of a sudden. Even foreboding.

Laura was starting to get an inkling of what it might have been that the assessors in the academy had seen in her.

"There's no one here," Laura muttered. She thought about it for a moment. "We need to get in there. Right now. Someone could be in danger. If the killer is preparing an attack right now—he might even lure someone to him, rather than visiting them. If that's the case, it's our duty to break the door down and get inside to save them."

Agent Moore looked back at her with what appeared to be a very clear understanding of what Laura was saying. "I can't be absolutely sure, but I think I may have just heard a scream," she said. "If that helps."

"It certainly does," Laura replied. She turned back to the door, analyzing it. Breaking down doors wasn't actually that hard. It was all about physics. You just had to use the right amount of force to hit the door at the weakest point—which wasn't going to be hard, since this one looked like it was made of mostly rotting and, in some places, warped wood—and then…

With the wrenching sound of splintering boards, the door burst inward and away from Laura's extended kick, leaving the entrance to the house open enough for the two of them to step through.

"Wow," Agent Moore said with a look that was not dissimilar to hero-worship on her face. It had the effect of utterly dispelling the increased confidence Laura had just started to feel in her abilities.

"Come on," Laura said. "We'd better look around, and quick. I'll go upstairs. Be careful. Keep your gun easy to access, just in case he is home after all."

Agent Moore nodded eagerly and sprang inside the house, pausing only to perform the proper safety checks before heading into the room on the left.

Laura tried to calm her racing heartbeat, telling herself that the rookie knew enough not to get herself in danger—and that she didn't believe anyone was home, anyway. In her experience, even people who were pretending to be out made some kind of audible reaction when their front door burst inward unexpectedly. It was going to be fine.

She moved up the stairs cautiously but fast, keeping an eye on the upstairs landing and twisting as she rose in order to check there was no one hiding in the spots she couldn't see. Just because the killer had been using a scythe didn't mean he didn't also have a gun. When she reached the top floor safely, she began to check each room in turn: a bathroom, which failed to manifest anyone standing behind her when she looked into the mirror. A bedroom, with the covers left in disarray from the previous night's sleep. A second, much smaller bedroom which appeared to be in use as some kind of study, though the furniture was sparse and cheap-looking.

That was it; the home was small enough for Laura's search of the first floor to be concluded in minutes, and it was deserted. She raced back down the stairs to check on Agent Moore and found her just coming out of what looked like an open living room/dining room, with a small two-seater sofa crouched in front of a television.

"No one," Agent Moore said. "You?"

"Nothing at all," Laura replied. "You didn't come across a basement door?"

Agent Moore shook her head. "I did find something interesting, though! Come look!"

Laura followed her across to the coffee table, which at first seemed to be strewn with a mess of different papers—most of them bills or unopened mail. There was a packet right on top of the rest, however, which had been opened and the contents spread about, notable for the yellow company logo at the top of each page.

"What is this?" Laura asked, bending over them. She was careful not to touch the pages. There was a strong possibility that they might trigger a vision, but she couldn't risk contaminating potential evidence. She had touched the door, after all, and gripped the banister as she ran up the stairs, and that contact hadn't triggered anything. Besides, if they already had him, she didn't need to see anything more.

"It's a genealogy report," Agent Moore said. "I've seen them on these online ads—you just put in your info, send a swab with your DNA, and they can tell you about all of your relatives and your ancestry. I've always wanted to do one. I bet I have some Irish in me with this hair."

Laura glanced at her auburn locks without comment. "This is a list of local matches," she said, peering at one of the pages closely. "And one of them is circled. Red ink, no less."

"His next victim?" Agent Moore asked, her eyes wide with excitement and adrenaline and a little hint of fear.

"Very likely," Laura said, grabbing her phone out of her pocket. "We need to go, now." She called the Sheriff's station to get the address as she ran back out to the car.

"It's Agent Frost," she said, as soon as the line connected, dispensing with pleasantries as she hurled herself back into the driver's seat. "I need you to look up a name for me. And after I get off the line, you need to send someone to Allan McLean's registered address. He's got a broken front door needs watching until we secure the scene. Everyone else needs to converge on the address you're about to give me."

She switched on the engine and threw the car into drive, ready to hit the accelerator pedal hard as soon as the GPS loaded the address.

Laura barreled out of the car for a second time, narrowly missing a collision with a young man who must have been the most enthusiastic of the deputies. Behind him she saw the Sheriff and another deputy, a woman. It was nice to finally get to see the other people working out of the station for once, but there was no time to focus on that.

Time always seemed to slow in these situations. Details became more clear. There was an intensity to everything, to every moment. Laura could see crystal-clear, hear every sound. She saw the house in front of them, the staff they had available, and made the necessary decisions in what must have been mere split seconds.

"You two, around the back," she barked quickly, gesturing at the fastest deputy and Agent Moore. "Watch the exits, intercept anyone who tries to leave. You others, with me. Guns drawn. Be ready."

That was it—the whole of the briefing she had time to give. If the killer was inside the home, then the screeching of tires as two cars pulled up outside, one marked with the Sheriff's colors and one plain, would have alerted him to their presence. He would be on the move—or worse, taking his victim now because he knew they were about to stop him. They had to move, and now.

Laura wasted no time, rushing to the door and hammering on it quickly. "FBI!" she yelled, as loud as she could. "For your own safety, open the door and show us your hands!"

There was a pause, and Laura decided she didn't want to wait any longer. Anything could be happening in there. Maybe the next victim was being held hostage. Maybe the scythe had made the first slash and he was bleeding out, waiting for the medical help that could save his life in only the next ten seconds. She checked out the door; it was stronger than the last one, better built, but nothing that she couldn't handle. She would have to take it. She took a step back, gearing up—

And nearly rushed right inside when the man opened the door, a startled expression already on his face.

His look didn't improve when Laura shoved past him and down the hall, shouting an order at the Sheriff to keep him contained. She moved into the kitchen with her gun pointed ahead of her, where there were two coffee mugs on the counter, one of them spilled—like someone had dropped it and run—there was movement—the back door was swinging open—

And Agent Moore stepped inside, pushing another man who looked scared half to death in front of her.

"He tried to run," she reported cheerfully. She had his hands in a vise grip, clicking a pair of handcuffs over them as though it was something she had done a thousand times before. She didn't appear out of breath or flustered in any way. It was like she'd only been out for an afternoon stroll and bumped into a friendly neighbor.

"Excellent," Laura said, with relish. She did like it when they tried to run. It made it that much easier to get the confession out of them in the interview room. A guilty person didn't try to escape the police. "Allan McLean, I'm arresting you on suspicion of murder. Agent Moore, read him his rights and get him in the car."

After what had felt like a long and difficult beginning to the case, they had finally gotten their man. That had been so easy!

Almost too easy, Laura thought, with a unwelcome shiver of doubt running down her spine.

CHAPTER TWENTY SIX

Laura sat down in front of Allan McLean at the table in the single interview room, next to Agent Moore, carefully covering her wince when the flimsy chair creaked. It looked as though this place didn't get a whole lot of use. She put a cup of fresh coffee down in front of herself, far back enough to be out of reach of their suspect, and opened the folder she'd brought in with her to start looking over the case notes.

"I haven't done anything," McLean said, before he'd even been prompted.

Inside, Laura almost cackled with glee. He was one of *those* suspects. The ones who would talk to fill the silence. All she was going to have to do was give him room to speak, and he would end up incriminating himself—or maybe giving a full confession. Wonderful.

Outside, she remained stoic and calm. She shuffled through the pages a few more times, then finally deigned to look up at McLean. He looked nervous, sweat popping on his brow, his eyes wide and desperate. His dark hair was ruffled and out of place, even though his hands were cuffed in front of him.

"Let's start with the motivation behind these murders," Laura said, keeping her tone even and cool. Like they were discussing a known fact and there was no point in him even trying to deny it. "That's what interests me the most. It's all linked to what happened back then, isn't it?"

She kept her words vague on purpose. She didn't want to be accused of leading him into a confession; she wanted it to come from his mouth alone. But she gave enough that he would know what she was talking about. He would have to know.

"What?" He gaped, then shook his head. His eyes flashed wide with surprise and shock. "I don't know what you mean. Back when? I don't have any motivation, because—because I didn't commit any murders! I've read about them in the paper but—but that has nothing to do with me!"

Laura sighed as if disappointed. "You know, you'll get a much more lenient sentence if you cooperate now," she said. "You have the death penalty here in Ohio, don't you? But you can probably get it reduced to life in prison if you talk to us. The more you resist and deny, the more likely it is that you'll get the worst possible sentence."

"No one's been executed here in years, anyway," McLean muttered. Then his eyes flashed. "But that doesn't matter, because I didn't do it! I'm innocent—I am!"

"You know a lot about the Ohio criminal justice system, don't you, Mr. McLean?" Laura said casually, leafing through her notes and bringing up the list of his prior convictions. "You did... let's see... three years, five months in the state prison, didn't you?"

"I..." McLean's face darkened. "I did, but that was then. I'm straight these days. I haven't been in trouble since I got out. I've been keeping my head down."

"That must have been hard work," Laura commented. "All that anger, that frustration—and I'm sure it was hard, getting back to life on the outside. Fewer opportunities for a man with a criminal record. So when all of that pent-up frustration came out, it must have really exploded. The kind of brutal violence that would impress even some of your old cell-mates."

"No," he said, shaking his head. "I mean, yes, it's been hard. But I've been staying calm. I took anger management courses in prison. I'm a changed man. I know how to get rid of the aggression without using my fists now."

"Right," Laura agreed. "Using a scythe."

"No!" he burst out, with a look of horror.

"Alright," Laura said, casually, as if it didn't matter to her either way. "Let's talk about something else. There was a genealogy packet on your coffee table. You traced your ancestry recently and found out who your nearest relatives are."

"Yes," he said, frowning. "I didn't think that was a crime."

"It isn't," Laura said. "But it's very interesting that you were looking up who was in your local area. Because three of the people listed in that packet are now dead."

"That doesn't prove anything," he argued. "There was a whole page of people in the area, and they're all related to each other, too. It could have been anyone else off that list. It could even have been a coincidence. There's a lot of farming families here have been around for a long time, generations get interbred and crossed. You could throw a stone in the center of town and hit someone who's related to me."

"Alright," Laura said. "So, you tell me why you were looking up your ancestry, then."

"Because I was curious!" he said. Then, seeing that it wouldn't be enough of an answer from her expression, he shook his head in frustration. "There was this big thing—this ancestors reunion event. I got a call from my cousin asking if I was going, and it was the first I'd heard of it. Turns out I wasn't invited because of my record. I just... I felt left out. I wanted to know."

"You already have a cousin that you know," Laura pointed out. "Why wasn't that enough? Or why couldn't you ask him to introduce you to people if it was that important?"

"He didn't go either," McLean sighed. "He thought it was dumb. But I... since my parents both passed, I don't really have anyone. A couple of aunts, couple of cousins—but we've never been all that close. I just wanted to meet people who were like me. People who might want to get to know me. I wanted family. He's a second cousin of mine, it turns out, and I just wanted to know him. "

"You circled a name in red pen," Laura said, moving to put a piece of paper across the desk in front of him. It was a scan of the real thing—the sheet with all the names. "Can you tell me why?"

"He's the one who responded to my messages," McLean said. "He agreed to meet me for a coffee. That's what we we're doing today. God... he probably won't want to know me now, either, after what you did!" He looked down at the table, as if upset.

"After what I did?" Laura repeated, and laughed. "What about what you did?"

"I told you, I didn't do anything!" McLean protested.

"Then you tell me why an innocent man with nothing to fear saw the police and ran," Laura said, leaning forward, propping her head on her hands as she eyed him keenly. This was the moment. She could break him here, she knew it. She could get him to tell her everything.

"Because...!" he exclaimed, then covered his face with his hands. When he spoke again, his voice was muffled. "Because I thought you were going to take me to jail."

"How prophetic," Laura said.

"No," he said, raising his head again. "Not for that. Because... I missed my last probation check-in. I'm supposed to attend all of them or they could put me back inside. I thought you were coming to do that."

Laura looked at him for a long moment. His posture was slumped, his shoulders down, his head lolling low on his neck. He was looking at the table. Not because he was trying to avoid her gaze, but because he was looking inward, feeling sorry for himself. If he was a liar, he was giving the best performance she had ever seen.

"Why did you miss your check-in, Allan?" she asked. "Were you too busy attacking other people from your genealogy packet?"

"No!" he said, wiping the heel of his hand stubbornly across one eye. He seemed resigned now. He probably thought he was done for no matter what, because of the probation violation. "I didn't even know all the victims recently were related to me. They weren't in the pack, not all of them. And I was just... I just slept in. I've got no one to wake me if I sleep through my alarm. I just slept in."

Laura considered this, leaning back in her chair. She knew she had to make some checks. If he was telling the truth about the genealogy pack, then they would have a hard time using it as evidence. That was bad news.

Unless he was telling the truth about all of it, in which case they had a lot more work to do—and fast.

Laura got up, beckoning Agent Moore with her. She left the room, glancing back to see Allan McLean with his head in his hands, not even watching them go.

A short walk down the hall, where she didn't think he would be able to hear them anymore, she turned to Agent Moore. "We need to check that packet right away, see if he's right about the results not showing all three victims," she said.

Agent Moore nodded. "I was going to check now," she said. "It's a lie, though, isn't it? Or just a half-truth because he knew they were related anyway? It has to be, because he's the killer."

"Is he?" Laura asked thoughtfully.

"It all fits," Agent Moore insisted. "He lives alone and he hasn't been able to find work since leaving prison, so he doesn't have any alibis for the murders. He has a history of violence and he had the information in his genealogy pack about who to target. We even caught him red-handed going after the next victim, about to lure him outside somehow so he could finish the job. And he has the right lineage for it. It has to be him."

"Hm," Laura said. She still wasn't convinced, even if the rookie was. She needed more than that. So would a judge. A jury might see their way to connect the dots, but they might need more to even bring it to court. A smoking gun, so to speak.

Something that he couldn't explain away with these coincidences and sob stories.

130

"Let's look at that information packet," Laura suggested. She moved to the nearest flat surface, a table which held a coffee machine and a tower of polystyrene cups, and laid her file on it. Sifting through the first pages which held information about Allan McLean and the murders, she found the photocopied packet and roughly divided the papers in half, handing one pile to Agent Moore.

"Here's Janae Michaels," Agent Moore said, after a few beats. They continued flipping through the pages in silence, each of them scanning every page.

"I've got Hank Gregory," Laura said, setting the page aside.

They both finished their last page and then looked up at each other, waiting. "Nothing for James Bluton," Laura said.

"Not in mine, either," Agent Moore said, sighing with frustration. "Why? What does that mean? Is he not related to them after all?"

"No, it just means the ancestry service McLean used didn't have his data," Laura said. "He may have requested they don't hold it, or it might just be a blind spot where they couldn't find the right records to confirm his identity. Or, in fact—this is a list of local relatives, and didn't that old farmer who found him tell us that he'd lived out of the area for a bit?"

"That's right!" Agent Moore exclaimed, snapping her fingers. "Fine. But it still doesn't rule him out, does it?"

"No," Laura said, reaching to gather the papers again. Her head ached a little as she brushed her fingers over the edges of the pages—

She was there again, in the past. There was a feel to it that she was starting to recognize. A sense that she was looking into an old photograph, a sign like sepia toning or age spots, something to the quality of the vision that she could neither fully put her finger on nor explain. But it was there, and she knew where she was even as her eyes opened on the scene.

The farmers, the screams, the same as before. An old man chopped down with the scythe before he could manage to get up enough speed with his walking stick. Then a young man, and—

The vision changed from its previous course, taking her backwards. She flew over the head of the killer as he raced toward his next victim. She knew him now, a man with dark hair dressed in the same style as the others, a scythe wielded to deadly effect in his hands. A farmer like his victims—his family.

She soared over it, going backwards fast, over the body of the young man, over the body of the old man. Back, back, back, up over the

131

hill that the killer must have come over, the place where the running farmers had first spotted him. Up and over, and then...

Back, over another field. There was a man lying on the dirt path, throat cut into a second smile that gaped horribly, front of his body slashed to ribbons. Strangely, Laura thought, he looked as though he'd been running in the opposite direction. Not away from the place the killer must have come from, but toward it. Why would anyone run toward a killer?

And then she soared over the body of the young woman and knew. His wife, maybe. His sister. Even his adult daughter—it was hard to gauge their precise ages through all of the blood.

Her vision soared up, up, up. Far in the distance she could see them, like stick figures and yet somehow also clear enough that she could identify what she was seeing. Like it would feel if she recognized someone she knew and loved at a distance, she supposed. She saw the bodies again where they had fallen. The young woman. The old man. The younger man. Far beyond him, toward the next homestead, there was another woman fallen, perhaps approaching her middle age. Then beyond her, the third man that Laura had seen running. Even he had not made it far enough away. Beyond him she saw the killer, soaked in blood, still marching determinedly toward his next victim.

She stopped inside the vision, hovering, looking over the scene. It was like her mind was telling her there was nothing else to see. That was it.

That was it...

Laura blinked, clearing her sight as she looked down at the pages of the open file.

"I have an idea," she said, which was true, even if she couldn't say where she'd gotten it from. "We need to talk to Alice again."

CHAPTER TWENTY SEVEN

Laura paced back and forth in front of their adopted desks as she waited for the line to connect, chewing on one of her fingernails.

"Hello?"

"Ah! Ms. Papadopoli," Laura said, yanking the nail out of her mouth. "It's Agent Frost. Can you do me a favor? I need to see some pages from your ancestry book. Do you have a scanner there?"

"No, I don't," she said, but then paused for a moment. "I do have the original PDF versions of the pages that I sent to the printer."

"Good enough," Laura said. "I have certain pages I need you to send over. The massacred family tree, and then the one with Ebediah Michaels and all of his descendant pages. Got that?"

"I'll send them as soon as I can get them uploaded to my email," Alice said, with a business-like tone which Laura very much appreciated.

"What are you expecting to find?" Agent Moore asked, as Laura hung up and thanked her.

"I don't know yet," Laura said. "It's just a theory—I can't be sure."

"Will it prove that Allan McLean is the killer?" Agent Moore asked. "Did you figure something out about his background that he won't be able to deny?"

Laura glanced at her sideways. "No," she said. "No, I don't think it's him. I know you're convinced, but I have a feeling... I can't explain it, exactly. I just don't think it's him. I believe his alibis and excuses."

Agent Moore frowned, the expression turning into a little pout. "But it *is* him," she said. "We found him just about to kill his next victim!"

"Was he?" Laura asked. "He had no weapon on him. We know the killer uses a long-bladed weapon, so it's not as though he could just use something from inside the house. And he sat down to have a coffee with his supposed victim, which would be a huge change in his MO—the killer just lures them outside and takes them out. Even this distant cousin of his swears it was all innocent."

"But he wouldn't know, would he?" Agent Moore asked. "The cousin. And maybe he was doing a kind of recon, working his way up to the murder. We know Hank Gregory was supposed to be meeting some new relatives he'd only just met. Maybe that's how he does it. Gets to know them first so they'll come outside when they see him."

Laura shook her head. "Sorry, kid," she said. "I'm just buying everything he says. Either he's not the killer, or I'm more naïve than I thought."

"I'm not a kid," Agent Moore complained. "I'm not that much younger than you."

Laura gave her a look. "What were you doing with your life nine years ago?"

Agent Moore frowned, tossed her auburn ponytail over her shoulder. "I was in high school, studying. Obviously."

"Well, then, you were in high school and studying when I went through the FBI entrance exam," Laura said. "So, to me, you are a kid. And you've got a lot to learn."

Agent Moore folded her arms over her chest, a flare of pink starting high up in her cheeks. "I'm not stupid just because I'm young," she said.

"Alright." Laura shrugged. "Well, if you're not stupid and you're sure that we have the killer already, then you can stay here. I have an inkling of who the real killer might go after next. Once I check the genealogy records and I have a name, I'm going to go and watch them, make sure they don't get attacked."

"And I get to continue the interview and try to get him to confess?" Agent Moore asked, her eyes lighting up.

Laura shrugged again. "If you like," she said, turning away at the sound of a ding from her computer. An email alert.

Truth be told, she had deliberately pushed Agent Moore toward an opposing position. Normally, the rookie was all too accommodating, happy to follow Laura around wherever she went. This time, that wasn't going to work. She need them to be at odds so Agent Moore would stay here, while Laura went out.

Why? Because she couldn't explain otherwise how she knew which person to protect. There was no way anyone could know what she did unless they were there. Since she couldn't come out and say that she'd seen a vision of the past, she was going to have to lie now and then think of something really good to make up later.

She read through the email attachments quickly while Agent Moore happily skipped back out to the hall. Laura had something much more important to focus on. If she was still harboring any belief that Allan McLean was the killer, she wouldn't have allowed Agent Moore to go in there alone—but as it stood, the timing and the content of that last vision had convinced her otherwise.

She needed to do this alone. Agent Moore would be fine, and she would get a bit of solo experience to make her less green. A win all around.

She pored over the file which showed the victims of the original massacre, trying to think. There had been an order to the deaths she saw in her vision. A young woman first. Searching the names and dates, she saw a twenty-five-year-old who had died on that day nearly two hundred years ago. And how old had Janae Michaels been? Laura checked her notes. Twenty-five.

Then there was James Bluton, who was in his thirties—several of the young men matched up with his age, but most notably was one who was listed as the husband of the young woman who had died. The most likely to be running toward her to try and save her life, of course.

The third victim in modern times had been an old man—Hank Gregory. The two who had died back then—their father was also one of the victims of the massacre. He'd been older, too. Old enough to match.

She had it.

There was a pattern here—one she wouldn't have seen without her visions of the past.

The killer must have known something about the original massacre, too. He must have access to some kind of firsthand document—perhaps a report from the local authorities at the time, or an eyewitness account from the sole survivor. Once, Laura might have thought that there was a possibility he was seeing visions of the past, too. In all her years of searching, though, she had still never found anyone who could do what she could. She was no longer willing to even consider it. Not only was it too heartbreaking to be let down time and time again, but it was also chilling to consider she might share an ability with a killer.

But this was good. This, she could use. The vision had shown her what happened next: a woman, in her forties or so, she had thought. She consulted the chart of those killed in the massacre and, yes, there she was. A woman from a separate arm of the family, a cousin to the three who had died first. She was next. That meant there had to be someone who was the modern-day equivalent, someone from the killer's bloodline who was around the same age.

Laura checked the pages Alice Papadopoli had sent over, and there she was. A forty-five-year-old woman who lived on the outskirts of town. Hannah Martinez, who must be from a branch of the tree that had at some point married into Hispanic blood.

She was just a name on a piece of paper—a birth date with no death date next to it. A woman alone, no spouse, no children. But Laura knew she was more than what the pages could say. She was a woman. A human. Someone with hopes, dreams, aspirations, relationships.

She was the next victim.

Hannah Martinez was going to die today—unless Laura could get over there in time to save her.

CHAPTER TWENTY EIGHT

He sat outside the farm and waited, watching her moving about through the windows. She'd only just come back from a long day at work in the fields and running errands in town. She'd soon be taking on new laborers—he knew that, because he'd seen the ad she was drafting up for the local newspaper on the screen of her laptop through the kitchen window. Now was his chance, and it was good that she hadn't had the time to bring anyone in. It made things perfect for him.

No husband around to protect her, now that he was dead. No children to get in the way. He didn't want them to have to see the unspeakable horrors of their parents' deaths, either—even if he was going to have to take care of them, too, eventually. That could happen further down the line. They weren't able to have children of their own, yet—but the parents still were. Besides, the children were killed later in the day. That was when Ebediah Michaels, having completed his bloody work in the fields, went into the homes and waited for the children to return so that he could make sure he left no soul intact.

He'd been mistaken, of course, in thinking that his duty had been done. But that made his crime no less heinous. No less worth atoning for.

Evil was evil, pure and unchangeable. It couldn't be allowed to live on as it had. Not even in those innocent children, who would grow up one day to be something else entirely if left unchecked.

He could see her more clearly now, as the light of the sun slowly disappeared from the sky. She had the lights on in her kitchen, where she'd eaten alone. The children, he'd gathered, were with their grandparents. It might not be so easy to get to them now, but he could think about that later. Perhaps with the grandparents thinking all the trouble was happening here in town, they might let their guard down. Imagine that the children were safe. That would help him immensely.

Focus, she told him. *You're getting too distracted. You told me it would be fine for you to take care of the children. Was that a lie?*

"No, no," he muttered quietly. "I'll do it. I just get bored. These long stretches of waiting and watching. I just like to plan ahead."

Stop thinking about the future so much and focus on what is right in front of you, she whispered, making him raise his head and look again.

The woman—she was done for the night. Taking a big glass of red wine and draining it empty, setting the glass down by the sink and leaning her hands on the counter for a moment, processing. She raised her head and looked out over the fields like a ghost of a woman. So sad and empty. It made him shudder a little.

Don't feel sorry for her now, she hissed at him. *Remember she wouldn't even be here if what happened to me had turned out differently!*

He nodded silently, just to let her know he had heard and he agreed. He wasn't going to back out now. Besides, she wouldn't be sad anymore once she was dead. It was a kindness, really.

He crept forward, staying level with the low hand-built stone wall that separated one of the field boundaries, keeping her in his sights. He needed to make sure she moved to where he needed her. He could have broken in, attacked her inside the farmhouse, but that wasn't right. That wasn't where it had happened.

He moved out into the field, crossing the open space quickly, out near a side of the house where the kitchen had no windows. He couldn't see her, but she couldn't see him. It was the shortest time he could dare to take without seeing her, unsure otherwise if she would do what he needed her to.

He crouched against the stone wall of the farmhouse, took the sizeable rock he'd picked out earlier and carried in his pocket, and threw it hard against the old stone well that sat near the kitchen. It made a loud clatter, and though he couldn't see her now, he thought he might be able to picture her: standing at the window, eyes straining into the darkness, trying to make out whether there was someone out there.

There was a long pause; he was about to reach into his pocket for another stone, but then he heard it. The kitchen door opening out onto the night, allowing her to step outside. And another sound—the *ch-chink* of a shotgun being pumped.

"Whoever you are out there," she yelled, which meant he was getting to her, even if she was trying to brave her way through it, "I've got a gun and I'm not afraid to use it. This is private land. You better get yourself back to the road and get gone."

There was a long pause. He heard a couple of footsteps and tensed, but there was nothing else. He had to do something to make sure she didn't just go back inside the house.

He took one of the stones out of his pocket and dropped it against the wall, letting it clatter down against the front of the house, just along from where she must have been standing.

138

"Right!" she yelled, and he heard her coming toward him.

He smiled to himself. He'd been right. He had thought that she was the kind of woman who wouldn't just back down and run. The kind of woman who wouldn't cower inside the house and call the police. No, she was proud and headstrong, willing to risk being killed in order to protect her home and her family. With the death of her husband so fresh in her mind, she was liable to fire that gun at anyone who so much as looked at her funny.

Her feet crunched on the ground as she came near to him, and he raised the scythe, ready to strike her as soon as she turned the corner. Even if she was cautious, even if she came leading with the barrel of the shotgun first, it didn't matter. He could slash the thing out of her hands before she had the time to aim and fire it.

Her footsteps stopped, and so did his heart for a moment, thinking she wasn't coming to come his way at all.

The moon had come out from behind a cloud from behind him, and he hadn't thought of that, had he? He hadn't considered that as the days went on, the moon was getting brighter, closer to full. So curious that *she*, who had lived back in a time when the moon was the only light you might expect at night if you couldn't afford a candle, hadn't brought it up.

But it didn't matter who was to blame. Because she was pointing the shotgun at him now, and she pulled the trigger.

There was a click.

An empty click.

Nothing happened.

He stared at her for a moment, her eyes wide—but without warning she was running now, and he sprinted forward, trying to catch her.

Trying to get to her before she went inside.

She was scrambling at the door as he raced down the side of the farmhouse, gasping at something, tugging at something that wouldn't move. The lock. The lock wouldn't open! He couldn't believe his luck!

To almost lose her because he hadn't thought about something as simple as the moon casting the shadow of his scythe on the ground in front of him, and then to have the chance handed back to him because she was accidentally locked out of her own home!

She turned desperately and started to run again. In the confusion she'd dropped the shotgun while she tried to wrestle with the door, and he almost tripped over it. Now THAT would have been some luck! To trip over the very discarded weapon that left her now defenseless!

He leaned into his stride, pushing himself to run even faster after her, knowing he had the stamina to catch her before she could outrun him or get away to a safe place.

All he had to do was keep chasing, and she would fall before his blade.

CHAPTER TWENTY NINE

Laura dove out of the car as soon as she was able to stop, racing toward the front door of the house and reaching for her weapon as she did so. She was growing more and more concerned with every moment that the sun dipped lower and lower toward the horizon. Even though the moon was set to be bright tonight, it only played on her nerves more.

The killer didn't wait until dark to strike. He did it whenever it pleased him. Could she really have managed to get here in time?

Wasn't it more likely that the woman she was here to save was already dead?

She knocked on the door too loud, too fast, casting glances around at the darkening scenery as she did so. She had a bad feeling, a terrible unease that was settling over her like a veil. She was beginning to be sure that she was going to have to go around the back and find a body.

Then the door opened, leaving Laura standing there in surprise, one hand still lifted to carry on knocking.

"Hello?" she said, blinking.

"Hannah Martinez?" Laura asked, glancing behind her into the corridor to see if she could spot anything unusual that might give the game away. Maybe the killer was here. Maybe he was somewhere in the backyard already, waiting to lure her outside.

"Yes," the woman at the door said, looking Laura up and down with utter confusion. "Sorry, what's this about?"

Laura got out her badge and showed it to her, glancing around the fields and the road behind them nervously. "I need to come inside," she said. "I'm sure you were called by the Sheriff's department recently and warned to stay inside your home or with a friend at all times?"

"Yes," Hannah said again, stepping to the side to let Laura in. "Yes, my sister's here. We decided to stick together for a few days until this is over."

Laura moved into the house, walking down the hall in search of this sister. She emerged into a cozy living room by instinct; on the sofa, a woman with an obvious family resemblance was staring up at Laura with an expression of confusion that matched her sister's.

"Good, you're both here," Laura said, noting to herself that the sister appeared younger, as expected. Out of the killer's age range. That didn't mean he wouldn't try to get two for one, though. "Have you seen or heard anything unusual today? Any noise out in the yard that you were tempted to check out?"

"No, nothing like that," Hannah answered, following her into the room. "Have we, Millie? Nothing has happened here. We were just wondering whether anything *was* going to happen."

Laura turned to her rapidly. "It's of the utmost importance that you continue to shelter together and stay inside," she said, her words coming out like a spray of automatic bullets. "I mean it—don't go outside under any circumstances. You really haven't seen or heard anything?"

"Nothing," the sister confirmed, dropping the cell phone she was holding onto her lap. "Do you think we're at risk?"

"Yes," Laura said, bluntly. She turned in a circle, trying to think. This didn't seem right. Something was off. Her instincts, which after all *had* been honed by years of FBI work as well as the very real clues from her visions, were telling her that something was wrong here.

Like maybe she was in the wrong place.

"Let me just think," she said, tapping her own phone against her chin. She'd gotten it right, hadn't she? She'd found the woman in her forties who fit the bill of what the killer was looking for. That was what she needed, wasn't it? What the killer needed?

But... there was one thing she hadn't really considered. She hadn't continued her search after finding Hannah. She'd allowed herself to get too excited and rushed out to save her, knowing the clock had to be ticking down.

But Hannah was safe. Protected by her sister. Not a good target. Difficult for the killer to get her alone, and if he had to kill the sister too, that might force him to move out of the correct order and ruin his carefully constructed plan.

Laura paced back and forth for a moment, racking her brain for an answer. She turned on her phone screen, flipped through her emails to read the PDF files Alice had sent again. She scanned the pages, trying to make them make sense.

"Hannah," she said. "I just want to check. Your parents are Joaquin Martinez and Beverley Martinez, born Beverley Brown?"

"Yes," Hannah said, then frowned slightly. "Well, I mean, they're our real parents. The people who raised us."

Laura froze and looked at her. "Why did you phrase it like that?" she asked.

"Because we were adopted," Hannah said, glancing at her sister. "Me and Millie. We were in care from when I was six, and our parents took us in to foster us at first. They ended up legally adopting us."

A growing sense of horror bore down on Laura. The killer, who knew enough to know the precise order in which to kill his victims to mimic the massacre... he wouldn't have missed a detail like this. He wouldn't have got it wrong.

There was nothing on Alice's pages about this. But then, she guessed there wouldn't have been any need to put it down on paper. Legally, Hannah and Millie were the daughters of the Martinez couple. That made them related, even if not by blood.

But it also made them no longer viable targets.

Laura wrenched her eyes back to her phone, poring over the pages to try and find another woman who fit the bill. There was no one. Everyone else was older or younger. They just didn't fit the age requirements.

Except—

Except Maria Bluton, currently forty-one years old, six years her husband's senior. But then, it all made sense, didn't it? She'd lived a whole different life before him, been married to someone else before they met. That abusive husband of hers who had ended up dead.

Forty-one. The same age as the woman who had died in the massacre. Laura had overlooked her completely before, knowing that her husband had already been targeted. Somehow, she'd crossed off their family in her mind. She'd seen Maria as a spouse only.

But now she remembered. Alice had pointed it out, hadn't she? They were distant cousins. Distant enough for it not to matter that they ended up married. They probably weren't even aware of the link themselves.

But the killer would be.

"I have to go," Laura blurted out, racing toward the door. "Keep doing what you're doing and you'll be fine!" She saw no sense in letting them relax, just in case she'd got their ancestry wrong as well, just in case it turned out that their natural parents were, after all, descendants of the same line. Because she'd gotten it wrong already once, hadn't she?

She'd gotten it so wrong that maybe she had just sentenced Maria Bluton to die.

Laura dialed her phone furiously as she slammed the front door of Hannah's home behind herself and jumped into the car, waiting impatiently for it to connect. It did so as she turned her key in the ignition, the engine roaring to life before she'd even put her seatbelt on.

"Agent Frost?"

"Agent Moore!" Laura called out. "No time to discuss—just listen. I need you to head over to the Bluton farmhouse right now. Get a deputy to drive you and bring back-up. Right now!"

"I'm on my way!" To her credit, Agent Moore was already ending the call before Laura threw the phone down. Then all that was left was for Laura to punch the accelerator pedal to the floor, paying no heed to the darkness or the uneven country roads as she sped as fast as she dared toward Maria Bluton.

CHAPTER THIRTY

Laura pulled up at the Bluton farm and leapt out of the car, leaving the engine idling, not wanting to waste even the moment that it would take to turn it off. She raced toward the front door in the darkness, almost tripping over a loose stone on the path. The house was silent, but the kitchen light was on. That and her headlights were the only illumination around.

There was no time to waste on knocking and waiting politely for Maria to answer the door. Laura tried it and found it locked, then raced around to the side in the direction of the lights, thinking she could get Maria's attention through the kitchen window. There was a door round there, too. Laura ran toward it—

And stumbled again, this time hitting the ground as she stumbled over something lying there in her way. Her hands groped for it blindly, her eyes adjusting to the darkness enough to make out a long shape as her fingers closed on it. The smooth metal was a familiar shape, the weight a known one when she lifted it.

A shotgun.

She should have been wearing gloves; maybe it was evidence. But it was too late now. She'd touched it, even the trigger. Useless for evidentiary value now. She kept her grip on the barrel firm, taking it with her as she stood and turned in a circle, straining her eyes for some sense of movement and her ears for a sound. All she could hear was her own engine rumbling quietly behind her. Damn. She should have turned it off.

Laura turned back to the kitchen door and fumbled with it, finding it locked as well. At least that was good. If Maria was inside, she was being sensible. But the discarded shotgun was giving her a sense of unease that crept all the way down her spine as she pounded heavily on the glass of the door, trying to get Maria's attention. She waited a moment and then did it again.

Nothing.

The night was almost silent, except for her damn rental car.

Laura blew out a heavy breath, then began to race around the side of the house, her eyes searching all directions as she went. Somewhere out here, there was a woman who was in danger.

145

Laura hoped beyond words that she wasn't about to stumble over her corpse.

She made it almost a three-sixty around the house when she heard the scream.

Laura froze for just one moment, her whole body going stiff with fear, all her senses straining to pinpoint the sound. There was a small copse of trees, the beginnings of a wood, right behind the home on the final side, the one not far from where she had parked her car, at a distance of maybe five hundred feet. That was where the scream had come from. She was sure of it.

Laura had no time to let fear rule her. She had to move. It was the only way she could help to save a life. That was her job—the duty she had sworn to complete when she signed up for this.

It didn't mean her heart didn't pound, her veins didn't freeze, her mind didn't flash into fight or flight mode immediately.

It just meant that, as she threw herself headlong toward the trees, she chose fight.

Laura only had a few brief and blissful moments of that open view on either side of her, that clear sight, until she plunged into the trees and the cover of darkness. It was like running headlong into pure night. The trees shaded the light from the moon, which was strong enough to illuminate her path when it was out from behind the clouds. But it was drifting under cover and out of it, a light wind pushing the clouds across it, and when it was covered it was blacker than tar under those trees.

Laura paused a moment, getting her bearings. Hoping her eyes would adjust more. If she lit up a flashlight, she would give her own location away, make herself a target. She might even lead the killer right to Maria, if she wasn't already dead.

She shoved the shotgun through the back of her belt, drawing her own gun instead. It was lighter, easier to run with, easier to aim at closer distances. In here, between the trees, there wasn't much room to maneuver. If she did come across the killer, it was going to be fast and unexpected. It was going to be close.

Laura couldn't wait any longer, couldn't waste any more time. Even though she could barely see much more than the few trees around her, Laura plunged further into the darkness of the woods, fighting her way through branches that threatened to snatch at her clothes and raise roots that threatened to trip her. She had no way of knowing if she was going in the right direction, only her memory of the scream and the rough area it had come from. She was relying on luck, on the

146

possibility of a vision, on something, anything. All she knew for sure was that she had to keep going.

Maria, Maria, Maria—the name raced through her head as she fought her way forward, all too aware of how much noise she was already making as she crunched twigs underfoot and snapped them off branches as they caught on her FBI windbreaker. She wanted to call out the name, to tell the woman she was coming. To let her know that help was at hand.

But she couldn't give away her position so easily. Not without putting herself—and the very rescue she was attempting—at risk.

She was making too much noise as it was. Every snapped twig could be the one that gave her away. She wasn't trained in moving quietly through woods like this, and even if she was, in the dark it would be next to impossible. The only thing she could hope was that it would be the same for the killer, that he wouldn't hear her over the noise he was making—

She stopped dead, realizing how stupid she was being. All she had to do was listen. Stop making noise of her own, and listen.

Laura strained her ears, looking around, her eyes as wide as she could make them even though it wouldn't help her see anything in the near-complete darkness. She listened. Just listened. Her own heavy breathing from her run, her heart pounding in her ears, the rustling of the breezes through leaves that were dry and dying—

There!

Laura turned toward the cracking noise she'd heard, forcing her body forward with all the strength she had, racing right through a tightly grown pair of trees whose branches interlocked. She felt the branches whip at her clothes, catching her hair in its ponytail, scraping over the bandage on her hand and threatening to tear it off. She thought she'd heard something else. Something that put even more fire into her steps, even more speed in her reckless headlong approach.

The quiet whimper of a woman's voice.

There was a chance that Maria was still alive.

Laura raced toward the sound, and she burst out into a small open clearing between the trees just as the moon came out from behind the clouds, leaving her a full view of the scene in front of her—

It was like a tableau before her eyes, her senses so heightened with the adrenaline surging through her veins that she took it all in at a single glance and understood everything.

There was the killer, a man she'd never seen before. He wore dark clothing, shrouding his face in a hood, a look that combined with the bloodied scythe he held to create a chilling image. A vision of Death himself. He looked at Laura as she emerged from the trees, his eyes swinging around, and she saw that he had a facial structure she knew. He was clearly related to Allan McLean—the same dark hair and eyes, the same long nose, the same mouth. He was younger, though. Maybe in his early or mid-twenties.

Maria Bluton was on the ground in front of him, struggling to crawl backwards, trying to get away from him. Her leg was bleeding heavily from a cut that had slashed through her jeans, the fabric already starting to drip, stained red from the wound downward. The ground was getting soaked with it, splashes sinking into the soil with every movement she made.

With a flash, Laura saw it all. The sickle ready to sweep down and harvest her, almost like she was an ear of corn ready to be slashed in half. The killer, his victim, the fact she was so close to losing her life. With a flash, she had her gun pointing in the right direction, aiming right at the killer's head, the range close enough that she wasn't at all concerned about not being able to hit him.

But with a flash, the killer, too, had seen her—taken it all in—and reacted. In the same moment she brought her gun to bear on him, his sickle slashed through the air toward Maria's neck, freezing just the moment before it cut her a second smile to match her husband's.

He stared at Laura. She stared back. On the ground between them, Maria sobbed once, then froze too, her neck having touched the sharp blade with the outward breath.

If she shot him, he was likely to cut her neck, the curved blade severing her arteries even as he fell.

If he cut her neck now, she would shoot him, killing him where he stood. They both knew that there was no chance she would miss at this distance.

They had themselves a stand-off.

"Well," the killer said. "What now?"

CHAPTER THIRTY ONE

"Now, you stop," Laura said, simple, authoritative. Somehow, despite her headlong run through the forest, despite the adrenaline and the fear, she kept her voice level and calm. The hand pointing her gun at his head did not shake. She had trained for this—not in the Academy, but in all the years since, every chase, every confrontation.

Every killer she had taken down.

This one had to be just the same as the others. There was no other option for her. Laura wouldn't accept the death of one more person at the hands of this man.

"Stop?" he repeated. His own voice was surprisingly level, too. She wasn't sure what she had expected. Hysteria was sometimes the way with killers who were caught in the act. Anger, snarling, aggression. Sometimes, abject fear at the fact that they had been caught. But this one—he was cool. There was maybe a little desperation under his tone, but not as much as she would have expected. It was almost as though he had known this moment would come, sooner or later. Planned for it. "I can't stop. You don't understand. I have to do this."

"How could you possibly have to do it?" Laura asked. "You're taking someone's life. There's never a good reason for that." Inwardly she knew that there were people, even in her own organization, who would disagree with her. Even her boss, Division Chief Rondelle, might frown at her for saying it.

There were times when you needed to kill. To save a life. Some would argue, to punish those who had taken the lives of others.

There was a strong possibility that if he didn't back down, Laura was going to have to shoot him herself. She would do what she could to avoid it—but not at the cost of Maria's life. Never at that cost.

"I have to," he said. There was a simplicity to his tone, a genuine belief that could not be shaken. A feeling that the reason should have been obvious, almost. On the ground between them, Maria whimpered again. "My ancestor commands me. Who am I to deny her justice after all these years? My own blood?"

Blood—Laura was all too aware of how much of it Maria was losing. They needed to end this sooner rather than later, one way or another. Laura needed to get her to a hospital. She would need stitches. Maybe, by the time she got there, a transfusion.

"You know that you're related to all of them, don't you?" Laura asked, her voice low. "Not just the survivors. The victims, too. You're all blood. Why make yourself as bad as Ebediah Michaels was, all that time ago?"

He snarled then, a dark look coming over his face at last. "I'm not as bad as Ebediah," he said. "I'm not. I'm balancing the scales. Restoring justice. Taking the lives of people who should never have been here in the first place. He should not have been allowed to live, to thrive, to father all these generations since."

"That doesn't make it their fault," Laura argued. "Do you think these people asked to be born as they were? That they wanted to be the descendants of a killer? They're innocent. Faultless. You're taking lives for no reason—for an injustice committed so long ago that barely anyone remembers."

"*She* remembers," he said, his voice a sharp snap in the night. "She's trapped here. Did you know that? Trapped by the fact that he got to live while her family did not. She had to spend the rest of her life without them. Had to grow old knowing she was the only one left— orphan, cousinless, not a single blood relative left other than her own children."

"And him," Laura reminded him. "Ebediah and his offspring. They were her blood, too."

He shook his head hard, like he was trying to dislodge a fly buzzing around his face. "No," he muttered. "No, I'm not listening. I won't let her change my mind. She's not going to sway me from you."

Talking to himself. Never a good sign. If his mind was unbalanced like that, Laura knew that Maria was in even more danger. If he wouldn't act rationally, they could be making the wrong gamble here. Maybe she should just shoot.

But if she did, she risked the blade coming up and taking Maria's life as it did so.

As a mother herself, Laura thought of Maria's children, already left without a father, and shuddered.

"These people can't be held responsible for something that happened almost two hundred years ago any more than you can," she said. "Why should this burden fall on you? It's not your fault you were born into this bloodline, either. Why should you have to give up your life for her?"

His eyes snapped onto her face from where they had trailed down to Maria. "I'm not giving up my life," he said, almost as though he was injured by the accusation.

"Of course you are," Laura told him. "You think you're going to walk away from this unscathed? We know who you are. Not just me. Others, too. The FBI. The local sheriff. We found you here by tracing your movements. We can do it again."

He frowned. It was a lie, but he didn't know that. It must have sounded believable for the way he faltered.

"Anyone would do what I did, in my position," he said. "I had to."

Laura realized with a growing sense of horror what his particular brand of self-deception was. They all had it, to some extent. Some killers believed they were so clever they would never be caught. Others knew they would go out in a hail of bullets and fancied it would turn them into a folk hero. This one—he truly believed he was going to get away with it. He must have pictured a courtroom, a jury of his peers all putting their hands up in the air and delivering a "not guilty" verdict. Like something out of a movie, deciding that even though he was clearly the killer it was so justified that he did not deserve punishment,

She didn't even think she had time to convince him he was wrong.

There was a sound somewhere nearby—near but not too near—a kind of rustling. Maybe an animal.

Maybe not.

"What's your name?" Laura asked, to distract him. She risked him figuring out that she had been lying earlier, but right now what she really wanted to do was to keep him talking while she figured this out. Maria was bleeding out—but she would do it a lot quicker if he moved that scythe in the wrong direction.

"Arthur McLean," he said.

"Allan's your... what? Cousin?" she asked. There was something moving between the shadows of the trees behind him. A darker shape amongst all the dark shapes. Laura tried very hard not to let herself look, in case he turned, keeping it in her peripheral vision only.

He blinked. "You know Allan?" For the first time, she noticed some uncertainty in his voice. He muttered to the side then, as if talking to someone else again. "No, I know, I'm not letting her distract me. It's just, if she shoots me I won't be able to carry on and do the rest. I'm doing this for *you*."

"I spoke to Allan earlier," Laura said, allowing some amusement to bleed into her voice. "I actually thought he was the one behind all of this, for a few moments. I realize now how wrong I was."

"Allan had nothing to do with this," he said quickly, forcefully. "It was just me and her, no one else. There's no reason to drag anyone else into it." Behind him, Laura could make out the faint glow of auburn hair hit by the moonlight. Agent Moore, stepping carefully out toward the open space of the clearing.

"Hmm," Laura said, pretending not to notice, even though her heart was racing faster and faster in her chest. "But they will be dragged in, won't they? This is about genetics. Everyone related to you will be under scrutiny. If not from us and the police, then certainly the world's media. A lot of people are going to have a lot of questions."

"That's not what I—" Arthur began, but then looked around quickly, and Laura cursed under her breath. He moved the blade so fast she couldn't do anything about it, clearly in response to the sound that she had also heard above his words—a crunch of another broken twig. Her finger twitched on the trigger of her gun but then she saw the blade hesitating at Agent Moore's neck and she stopped, unable to make a move again. On the ground, Maria stayed frozen, staring at everything in abject terror, her leg still bleeding out.

A different stand-off this time.

"Backup?" Laura asked quickly, needing to communicate with Agent Moore fast and get the reaction she wanted. There was a plan forming in her mind—a sketch of a plan only—an *if he does this, then maybe…*

"Behind me in the trees," Agent Moore said, her voice a strained gasp. She had frozen like a deer in the headlights with the scythe poised at her neck, the cruelly sharp blade curving around from one side and cradling her, the long edge of it pointing out across her other shoulder. Poised to slice her down in an instant. There was a thin bead of blood already running down across her collarbone where he had moved too fast to fully control the trajectory.

"Alright," Laura said. "Maria—go to the trees. Now."

"What?" Arthur said, his head whipping around fast. It was clear that he was losing control of the situation, that he was no longer running the show. "No! No, she stays!"

"You can't threaten all three of us at once, Arthur," Laura said, leveling her gaze at him. "If you're going to put that scythe at my partner's neck, then Maria goes." At her feet, Maria was already starting to move, scrambling across the earth for purchase, testing her leg to see if she could put weight on it. Laura knew the woman needed to get out of here fast, get treatment, or she wouldn't try a gamble this risky. But if it worked—

Arthur turned again, slower this time, his scythe leaving Agent Moore's neck for just long enough—

Laura pulled the trigger, hitting Arthur in the shoulder, her ears ringing in the aftermath of the shot. There was a moment of smoke and recoil and confusion and she didn't know if she had hit him or not, and then she saw the blood spray from his shoulder and the scythe leaving his grip, falling to the ground, narrowly missing the rest of Agent Moore's body to land—

To land safely, powerlessly, as Arthur clutched his shoulder and screamed, and then to her credit Agent Moore was pushing forward and grabbing his hands behind his back and pulling out a pair of cuffs to snap on as if she hadn't just had a weapon grazing her throat. By the time Laura had holstered her gun and stepped forward to kick the scythe far away, Agent Moore had him fully restrained, ready to be taken away.

"We're going to need a couple of ambulances," Laura yelled, loud enough for the deputies who were crashing loudly through the undergrowth now to hear. "Make it quick. There's a lot of blood loss."

Then she knelt, hurriedly undoing her belt to offer it as a tourniquet for Maria's leg, as Arthur screamed in pain and at the loss of his victim, his objective, knowing now as he must know that it would never be completed. Over their heads, shrouded by the darkness of the night and the branches of trees, birds that had been roused by the shot and the noise squawked and cawed out warnings, wings flapping into the distance to take them away, the woods transformed from dark silence to so much sensation that it was almost too much to take in.

CHAPTER THIRTY TWO

Laura slumped into one of the dark gray plastic chairs that made up the hospital's waiting room. Whenever she was in one of these, she always marveled at the deep lack of care on display by the hospital's builders. She knew from experience that sitting in one of these for any number of hours was liable to give you back pain and alignment issues, and an extra need for medical intervention than whatever you came in with.

Next to her, Agent Moore sighed deeply. Laura nodded, agreeing with the sentiment.

Laura looked up at her, swinging her head around where she had it propped on her hands, elbows on her knees, to examine the small white bandage stuck over her neck. "Does it hurt?" she asked.

Agent Moore shook her head no. "It didn't even need stitches or anything," she said. "Just feels like a scratch."

Laura nodded wearily. "That's good." It was nice to end a case without needing medical attention herself; a nurse had insisted on changing the bandage on her burned hand when she saw Laura pacing around and waiting, but it was hardly necessary. It was getting on its way toward healed just as expected, even if it was slow.

"Did you hear anything about Arthur McLean while I was gone?" Agent Moore asked. She'd tried to wait with Laura to see what the doctor would say, but she, too, had been strongarmed into getting her neck checked out by another nurse who wouldn't take "later" for an answer.

Laura nodded. "He's going to be fine," she said. "The Sheriff's deputies are all in there with him, and he's cuffed to the bed. The bullet went right through, so they just stitched him up and gave him painkillers."

"Are they getting backup soon?" Agent Moore asked, with a dubious expression on her face.

Laura laughed out loud, startling one of the other patients who had traipsed into the waiting room through the early hours of the morning as dawn rose outside. She lowered her voice again to reply. "Yes, there's a team coming from the nearest city to relieve them. I don't

154

think they've actually slept since this case started. Not that we ever actually saw them until right at the end."

"They're really overstretched here," Agent Moore said with total seriousness. "They should hire some more deputies."

Laura was about to present a teaching moment about state budgets and the local population versus the number of people who really wanted to be part of law enforcement, but she stopped. Agent Moore had taken a scythe to the neck last night, after all. And the night had been a long one.

"They should," she settled for, glancing up at the coffee machine on the other side of the room.

"Want a coffee?" Agent Moore asked, clearly seeing where her eyes had gone. "I'll get one. Call it my gratitude toward your amazing agenting skills."

Laura nodded, not wanting to invite further conversation on this point, and Agent Moore leapt up to skip over to the machine and feed coins into it until it spat out two insipid-looking coffees. She skipped back again, somehow not spilling them, and bounced right into her chair at Laura's side.

"I just don't know how you did it," she said enthusiastically, steamrolling over Laura's hopes that they wouldn't have to discuss it. "I mean, how did you figure out who he was most likely to go after next?"

"I didn't," Laura pointed out. "I went to the wrong place first. When the sisters told me they were adopted, I thought I'd been an idiot. Made the wrong guess. It was only luck."

"How could it have been luck alone?" Agent Moore asked, shaking her head. "You're too modest! I know you figured it all out. But how? Will you help me see how the pieces fit together? I'd love to be as good at this as you are one day."

Oh dear, Laura thought. She knew the truth. That Agent Moore didn't have a hope in hell of being as good at this as Laura was. That there was a basic, born-in instinct she was never going to have. Agent Moore was never going to have visions of the future—or the past— guiding her along.

"No, seriously," Laura said. "I just went to visit Maria Bluton to ask her some more questions about her husband, see if there was anything we'd missed. After my hunch about the next victim didn't pan out, I thought maybe there was some extra information she could give me that would help me out. When I got there, I saw the house deserted and the shotgun on the floor, and I knew something terrible must have happened."

"But you called me and told me to get over there with backup." Agent Moore frowned.

"That was after I arrived," Laura lied. "I knew something was off the moment I arrived. It took me a while to figure out where they'd gone, you see. I hadn't found them until just before you got there. It was only because Maria screamed when he finally caught up with her with that scythe—otherwise I might have been wandering through those woods all night."

She couldn't tell her the truth, of course. Just the same way that she'd never been able to tell anyone the truth. Until Nate.

Laura felt a clutch of pain in her chest at the thought of him. Her rightful partner. Being paired up with Agent Moore had turned out to be not quite as horrible as she expected—though it had had its moments—but still, it should have been Nate sitting next to her now. Nate who had her back when she was facing off against an armed killer. Nate making sure she got the treatments she needed at the hospital before she headed off to the airport.

He wasn't just her partner. He was her closest friend. And the loss of him, just at that moment, felt like something Laura didn't think she could stand any longer.

"Oh," Agent Moore said, frowning slightly. "It's just, I thought I could hear the background of the call... never mind. I guess I was listening for something that wasn't there."

"Probably just interference on the line," Laura said, smiling glibly as she sipped at the predictably horrible coffee. "Anyway, shouldn't be long now before we get the all-clear to head home. As soon as I hear from Rondelle, we'll head back to the inn and pack up, then over to the airport and back to D.C., just in time to not waste the whole of our Friday out here. You did good, kid. We got it done."

Laura had mostly expected Agent Moore to say something about not being a kid—in fact, she'd said it that way on purpose to distract her from the topic at hand. She was not prepared for the beatific beam that spread across the rookie agent's face, so wide Laura began to feel worried about the cut on her neck.

"You really think I did a good job?" she enthused, turning fully to face Laura by twisting in her chair, clasping her hands tightly around her own coffee. "That means so much, coming from you! Really, I thought it was you who did all the work, I was just getting in the way, and—"

"Alright!" Laura said, holding her hands up in the air in surrender. "Relax. Everyone's kind of useless when they're a rookie. You're less useless than most. It's a compliment. Now, try to be a little more chill, okay?"

Agent Moore nodded, bit her lip, and settled back in her chair. Laura immediately groaned inwardly. She didn't meant to upset the rookie, either. She didn't think she was very good at this part, herself.

"You don't have to be totally silent, though," she offered.

"Do you have any plans for the weekend?" Agent Moore asked, almost springing back up in her chair, as though she'd had the question loaded and ready to go.

"Yeah," Laura said, studying the empty cup of coffee. She wasn't even sure why she'd drunk the horrible stuff, except that she was going to need the energy. "I'm picking up my daughter from her father's place tomorrow morning. We've got a playdate tomorrow afternoon. And I'm going to call an old friend, see if he wants to meet."

"Sounds like fun." Agent Moore giggled. She opened her mouth, presumably to list off all of the things she had planned in return, but Laura's phone buzzed in her hand.

"It's Rondelle," Laura said with a grin, knowing that the flight home was now only a matter of hours away at most.

***

Laura grabbed Lacey's favorite unicorn toy before it could hit the ground, knowing that if it got dirty her young daughter would be inconsolable. "Just in time, sweetie," she said, giving her a knowing look. "Or Mr. Fluffy would have been going through the laundry."

"Uh-oh," Lacey said, blinking her huge blue eyes. Laura smiled and tucked her daughter's blonde hair behind her ears. She'd insisted on having her hair done up in bunny ears above her head—apparently, that was the style that everyone at her school loved. She'd only been attending for a few months, but already her social life sounded more exciting than Laura's own.

There was one standing date Laura had in her calendar, though— every time she had Lacey for the weekend, the two of them came here. To see Chris and Amy Fallow.

"Come on, then," Laura laughed, grabbing her daughter out of her car seat and putting her down on the sidewalk. As soon as her tiny legs had enough ground between them, she was off, toddling as fast as she could toward the door.

She'd barely managed to get one of her hands to slap the outside of the door, Laura still gathering toys from the back seat of the car and trying to catch up with her, when it opened. Behind it, Amy—about six months older than Lacey, but just as blonde and just as cute—waved enthusiastically and launched into a clumsy if affectionate hug. As the two little girls chattered excitedly about the day they were going to have and which toys they would play with, Laura noticed with a chuckle that Amy's hair was also in bunny ears.

"Hey," Chris said, standing back to let the girls pass by him, revealing himself as the taller and stronger figure who had opened the door for Amy to burst out. "You solved your case."

"I did," Laura said, stepping inside with her arms fully laden with unicorns, dolls and fluffy kittens and puppies. "Lacey insisted on bringing everything. She said they were having a toy reunion. She only knows the word because she heard me talking about the case on the phone yesterday and asked me what it meant."

Chris chuckled and took a few of the toys from her load. "No injuries this time?"

"No," Laura said, carrying everything over to the open-plan kitchen and family room space. The girls had already run over to Amy's toy box and were enthusiastically setting everything up in a circle, which they were clearly meant to join once it was completed. They were distracted, not listening. Laura took a risk, shooting Chris a glance. "Do you want to examine me to check, Doctor?"

Amusingly, Chris went a funny shade of pink that covered his ears and disappeared into his hairline, and he had to clear his throat. "I will trust your word for now," he said, though Laura thought he was quite pleased with the idea.

She was quite pleased with it herself.

They dropped the toys off with the girls, Lacey turning around bossily to move every toy Laura put down into a placement that was apparently more suitable for her. "Mommy," she tutted. "Unicorns have to go *next* to dragons, not opposite them."

"Oh, I didn't realize," Laura said, placing a hand over her chest in mock surprise. "How silly of me!"

"That's right," Amy confirmed. "And ponies go next to them on the other side. And we don't need any gross, kissy grown-ups!" She made a face like she'd just smelled something awful.

Laura looked at Chris. This time, he was going distinctly red instead of pink. "Um," he said. "Amy might have heard me talking on the phone to one of my friends about the other night."

Laura straightened up, away from the girls, and tilted her head at him. "You talk to your friends about me?"

Chris cleared his throat again, moving to the kitchen counter—probably as an excuse to cover up the awkwardness. From their usual seat at the island, they could watch the girls play without it feeling like they were cramping their style. A freshly made coffee was waiting for Laura—Chris was starting to know what she liked. It felt comfortable. Warm. Like home.

"Yes, well," he said, and shrugged. "Wouldn't you brag about the gorgeous Special Agent who manages to find the time in her extremely busy schedule of catching serial killers and jumping in the way of bullets to go on a date with you?"

Laura laughed, shaking her head at his flattery. "I'll let you know if it ever happens. But to be fair, I'm quite likely to brag about the handsome cardiologist known for his charitable work and new single dad who makes time for me. And by the way, I don't jump in front of bullets. It was blunt object trauma that gave me the concussion."

"Noted," Chris said. A shadow passed over his face for a moment when he glanced at Amy, and he sipped at his coffee. The usual smile he wore had slipped, but when he put the coffee back down, it was in place once again.

Laura frowned.

Was that a red flag she was seeing?

"Where did you just go?" she asked, bluntly. She'd known from the very start of her budding relationship with Chris that she had to be blunt with him. She'd only gotten to know him in the first place to protect Amy, after all.

Chris grimaced. "Sorry. It's hard sometimes. I guess I'm still not over it." He sighed. "I just... I knew my brother could be a piece of work. I just didn't think..."

"That it would go that far?" Laura supplied.

"Yeah." Chris sighed again, and shrugged. "I don't know whether that makes me a lousy judge of character, or just an optimist."

"Maybe both," Laura said. He looked at her with an injured expression and then laughed and shook his head when he realized she was teasing him.

"Look," he said. "I don't know if I'm a good judge of character. But I do know I want to see you again next week. I mean, you know. Without the girls."

Laura glanced over at the two of them, playing. It was like some kind of dream, something so distant from the alcoholic mess of her life only a year ago that it seemed impossible. One day, maybe, those two girls could be raised as sisters. Her daughter and his adopted one. She could live in this beautiful house, with a doctor husband and two beautiful daughters, watching them grow up, giving them everything they needed to thrive and overcome the difficulties of their early childhoods.

Something inside her rebelled at the thought, rejecting it firsthand without thought. But she knew what that thing inside of her was. It was the destructive, broken part of her. The part that wanted to drink until everything was gone. The part that still believed a girl like her, with the horrible ability that she had, should be quiet and hide away and never let herself go near another person in case she ruined their happiness.

It was her mother's voice, not her own. She was beginning to recognize that. She didn't have to keep all of herself hidden—even if, for now, she still wasn't at a place with Chris where she could show him that secret ability.

It was a beautiful dream. But maybe, if she wasn't getting too far ahead of herself, it didn't have to stay just a dream.

"I'd like that too," she said, smiling into her cup of coffee.

Her phone buzzed at her side, and Laura picked it up to read the message she'd been sent. It was simple, to the point. *I'll meet you at your place tonight.*

She hid it quickly before Chris could see, feeling her stomach drop at the thought of what was waiting later—trying to put it out of her mind so the anxiety wouldn't ruin the whole day.

CHAPTER THIRTY THREE

Laura checked in on Lacey in her bedroom, tucked up into her bed inside sheets printed with unicorns flying through fluffy clouds. A smile passed over her face at the sight of the tiny girl, her own features bathed in the soft glow of a nightlight on the dresser beside her. Laura often had to wonder to herself just how she and Marcus, who had turned out to be a pretty bad fit, had managed to produce something so perfect and sweet.

She turned away, setting the door to almost closed and padding back out into the living space of her small apartment. As always when she knew someone was coming over, she swept her gaze over everything with a critical eye: the battered old secondhand couch she still hadn't been able to save up enough to replace, the bare shelves, the lack of framed photographs. She'd left everything behind when Marcus threw her out. Most of her framed photographs had him in, anyway, and she hadn't wanted them.

Her home looked like what it was: a place where a recovering alcoholic was trying to rebuild her life. the only room that had seen any real attention was Lacey's room, and that was recent. It hadn't even been all that long since they'd come to a court agreement that allowed Laura to get custody on weekends. Laura had to pinch herself sometimes. She had spent a long time wishing for her life to come back together, and it really was starting to.

She paced the floor restlessly, clasping her hands together too tightly to be comfortable. She let go consciously, shaking her fingers in the air to dispel the discomfort, and turned to pace in the other direction only to find she was clasping her hands again. She hadn't been nervous like this for a very long time.

She had no idea what he was going to say. After she'd reached out to Nate and told him she wanted to meet up, over text, his reply had been so slow she'd begun to believe there wouldn't be one. And what he'd said—*I'll meet you at your place tonight*—was so ambiguous.

Was he annoyed? Done with her? Angry? Afraid? Ready to tell Rondelle everything and ruin her reputation?

Or what?

The knock on the door almost made her jump out of her own skin, a full-body flinch that made Laura realize just how scared she was about facing him. Telling him had been awful. Having him not believe her had been worse. And when he did believe her, the look of disgust on his face had been the worst yet.

Laura shook out her hands one last time and forced herself to stride to the door and open it, believing that faked confidence might turn into the real thing if she tried hard enough. She looked up, and there he was: her longtime partner, her confidant, her friend. Lately, her nightmare.

Nate Lavoie was taller than she was, making her tilt her head up at him. He filled her doorframe with a kind of unwanted presence, like he was wishing he could make himself small. His hands were shoved into the pockets of a dark hooded jacket against the cold, the hood itself up over his head and his neatly coiled short dark hair. He bit his lip when their eyes met, then made a kind of shrugging moue.

"Alright if I come in?" he asked.

Laura nodded wordlessly, not trusting her voice, and stepped aside. He entered, wiping his feet on the doormat, and paced across her floor, unknowingly taking the same route she had a moment ago. He paused and lingered in front of the television, as if not sure where to go next.

They weren't exactly friends outside of work. Not like that. Not when work was such a huge part of their lives that it was almost all there was. He was unfamiliar with her space.

"Sit down," Laura offered. "Would you... would you like something to drink?"

Nate gave her a startled look halfway to the couch.

"Like coffee?" Laura elaborated, hating that his mind had gone to alcohol right away. That was her own fault, she knew. She was going to have to spend a long time working on fixing it. But right now, that wasn't the issue. The issue was whether he was going to let her have that long time to know him in the first place.

"Yeah," Nate said, which was good because she figured it meant he intended to stay for a while. "Yeah. Coffee would be great."

"Lacey's asleep in the bedroom," Laura said, nodding her head down the hall. "She's a pretty good sleeper, but..."

Nate nodded back as she started the coffee machine. "I won't wake her."

Good. He wasn't going to storm out right away, and he wasn't going to shout. That was good progress. Laura faced the kitchen window for a moment, catching her breath, wiping her hands on the sides of her pants. She took out two coffee cups, remembered she'd had several with Chris, and put hers back in favor of a glass of orange juice from the fridge.

She took the drinks to the coffee table, set them down, and paused, realizing she'd left herself nowhere to sit. Nate was sunken into the worn cushions of her couch, looking almost ridiculous, his long and muscular frame getting swallowed up by that beat-up piece of junk. After a moment, Laura gave in to the inevitable and sat right next to him, awkwardly close for someone who might be about to tell her he didn't want her in his life anymore.

Nate picked up his coffee and sipped at it.

The suspense was almost killing her.

"So," he said, and she sat up straight, hanging on every word. "I've been thinking. A lot. I've had time to process what you told me. What you... showed me, I guess."

"And?" Laura asked, her heart so far up her throat that her voice came out breathy.

"And," Nate said, pausing for a moment. "And I think I can live with it."

"What?" Laura burst out, in unrestrained excitement. She'd been so sure he was going to say he was leaving. That she was never going to see him again.

"I spoke to Rondelle already, and he cancelled my transfer," Nate said. He glanced at her then, a look of alarm and uncertainty in his deep brown eyes. "Unless—unless you don't want that. Damn, I did that without asking if you still want to be *my* partner—"

"Of course I want to be your partner," Laura said. She was blinking back tears from her eyes. "Oh, god. Nate. I thought..."

He looked at her and Laura felt him seeing her, realizing. Seeing how much pain and uncertainty she had been in. How she had feared losing him forever, after all their years of being a team. "It's alright," he said, gently. But then he cleared his throat and his manner changed, shifted less personal again. "I'm still trying to, you know, fully reconcile what you told me. But I, um. I want to work through that while remaining as your partner, instead of running away."

Laura had to look away, pretending to examine her orange juice. If she didn't, she was going to break down and cry. She'd never had anyone know about her ability—not fully. Her parents, she knew, had kind of suspected when she was a young child. Any hint she'd shown of knowing the future back then had been stifled quickly, shoved down, and then never acknowledged again. Like she'd had an imaginary friend—not a gift.

163

But for the first time in her life, Laura had told her secret to someone—and he had remained an ally.

He was on her side.

"You won't tell anyone else?" she asked, because she had to be sure, because it would be terrible if his stipulation for all of this was that she had to come clean.

"Not if that's what you want." Nate shook his head, taking a long sip of his coffee. "I don't pretend to understand. It must be a heavy burden, having this kind of secret. If it was me, I think I would want to make sure a few people knew. People like my boss, knowing it could help out with cases. But it's your choice. If you want it to remain a secret, I promise it will."

Laura nodded. "I appreciate that," she said, clearing her throat to hide the fact that her voice had cracked. "When are you back off leave?"

"Monday," Nate said, giving her a wry look. "Rondelle is of the opinion I've had enough time off already, these past weeks."

"He's right," Laura said, to tease him, but there was a weight of warmth behind it. "I've missed you. You know he stuck me with two rookies?"

Nate nodded toward her hand. "I heard about the consequences, too. I go on leave for two cases and you almost get yourself killed."

Laura smiled, hesitantly, but it was real. "I guess I need you to stop me doing stupid things."

Nate opened his mouth to say something, closed it, took a breath, and opened it again. "And I guess you can stop me from doing stupid things now, too," he said. "Without having to beat around the bush and pretend like you don't know for a fact what the consequences could be."

Laura nodded. "Right," she said. She contemplated that for a moment. "It's going to be hard. Breaking the habit of a lifetime to actually tell someone what I've seen."

"You go somewhere sometimes," Nate said, suddenly. He was gazing into the distance like he was reliving a memory in his head. "You kind of switch off, just for a second, and then you're back. And sometimes when you come back, it feels different. I always thought it was just... I don't know. Your thought process. Like you were realizing something."

Laura nodded. There was not much to say. He had already worked out the truth: that what he was seeing was the split second for which she was gone, away in her visions, no matter how long it lasted inside

164

her head. "The headaches, too," she said. "They come from this. Whenever I see something, my head starts to pound."

"God." Nate shook his head. "I feel like an asshole. I thought you were just constantly hungover. Or going through withdrawal, I guess."

Laura's smile tipped the corners of her mouth but didn't quite reach her eyes. "I probably was, most of them."

Nate nodded. Paused. He drained his coffee cup and set it on the table, looking at her. "I should probably head home," he said. "I didn't want this to be too... too overwhelming. Not tonight. I just want to do this... slowly, I guess. I don't think I can handle all the information at once. Let's just see what comes up when it comes up."

Laura nodded at that, accepting. She would have accepted just about anything in order to keep him in her life. To go back to being partners again. This was nothing.

"Then I'll see you on Monday?" she asked.

"Monday." Nate nodded. He stood, then hesitated a little. "Look, I don't... want things to be weird between us, even with this new thing going on. I just think we should try and get back to normal, right? As normal as we can. We just go in Monday morning like none of this happened. I don't know. Like I've known for years. No awkwardness."

"No awkwardness," Laura promised. "I'll get you a coffee on the way in."

"From that deli near HQ that I like?" Nate asked, pausing on his way to the door with a half-smile.

"That same one," Laura confirmed.

Nate chuckled, low and so familiar it made her want to cry. "Nah," he said. "You bringing me a coffee first thing? That would require you being a morning person, and we both know you're not. No weirdness, remember? Get me lunch instead."

"Deal," Laura laughed, and then Nate was gone, closing her front door behind him with a brief nod.

Laura took a breath. A deeper one than she'd dared to take in a long while. He wasn't forsaking her. He wasn't leaving. He didn't hate her.

There were things they still had to work on, but they were going to work on them together.

It was all she could have asked for.

There was a weariness that had settled into her bones now, a kind of drop in her energy now that the adrenaline and the relief had worn off. Like it had been the only thing keeping her going all this time, just trying to get to a future reality where Nate had forgiven her. She was exhausted, beyond anything she'd felt for a long time. It reminded her of those nights when Lacey was just born, when the two of them were up every two hours all night and all day, just to keep her fed. Before everything had happened with the vision that had sent her over the edge, the drinking, Marcus, losing Lacey, fighting to get her back.

Laura stood and turned off the lights in the apartment one by one until there was only the light of the moon, coming through from the window that faced in the direction of the city. Sparkling lights fell across the way between here and there, visible from the height of her apartment. She admired the view for one moment, then turned toward her bedroom.

The knock on the door was so loud that she almost fell back through the window in shock, her hand going to her belt for a gun that wasn't there.

Catching her breath and shaking her head at herself, Laura moved over toward the door, thinking that Nate had probably just forgotten to tell her something. Or, a paranoid part of her brain suggested, he was coming back to tell her he'd changed his mind after all and wasn't going to be her partner ever again.

She shook those bad thoughts out of her head as well and opened the door, ready to find out what he wanted.

Except her breath caught in her throat, because it wasn't Nate standing there after all. It was an old man, one she did not recognize at all. A neighbor? She was barely home often enough to know them by sight. Someone else?

Someone sent by Governor Farrow?

Her blood froze. Even though he was behind bars now, he'd had the clout and the finances before to have someone break into her home and leave a threatening message. What if this was him finally managing...

"Laura Frost?" the old man asked. He had a kindly face, like he was someone's father. Or grandfather, even. Like he wouldn't hurt a soul. He was dressed well in brown slacks and a gray sweater vest over a beige shirt, like he'd picked out the most inoffensive outfit possible from a catalogue.

"Uh," Laura said, because all of that didn't mean she was sure he was someone trustworthy. She knew a trick or two, though—because suspects often used them on her. She didn't need to say she was before she understood the situation. "Who are you? Do you realize how late it is?"

"I'm sorry about the hour," he said. "But I've been drawn here to you. I don't get to decide when it happens, it just does."

Laura frowned at him. "Excuse me?"

166

She could have slammed the door in his face. He sounded like a nutjob. If it walked like a duck and quacked like a duck, it was probably a duck.

But something held her back. A strange kind of sensation in her fingertips, a tingling—and the fact that when she tried to explain her abilities to people like Nate, they thought the exact same thing. She knew that it was possible for someone to have some kind of sixth sense driving them—because she had one herself.

He looked at her with more confidence now, nodding. She noticed his eyes were a startlingly bright and clear blue against the white of his eyebrows. "You're Laura Frost, and I'm supposed to find you."

Laura's mind whirred. Her gun was in her bedroom, high up on a shelf above the closet, in a regulation storage box. Not the most subtle hiding place, but it wasn't hidden. It was just out of Lacey's reach. If she needed it, if he turned out to be someone who had been affected by one of her cases in the past, maybe even a criminal from years ago she had failed to recognize...

She would have it in a moment.

"Why?" she asked, which was the clearest way she knew how to get to the bottom of this and decide whether to let him in or lock the door and call for backup.

He looked at her then in the stillness of the night, those clear blue eyes piercing into her as if he could send his meaning directly through them and into her own without need for words. "You know what I can do, because you can do it to," he said, his words quiet but spoken with strength and clarity. "I don't want to say it where your neighbors could hear, but let's just say I knew what you and your front door both looked like before I got here. I know there's two cups on that table inside, and a green sofa with cushions that have seen better days."

Laura stared at him. Lacey was inside the house. He didn't know that—maybe—but Laura had to keep her safe. Inviting a stranger in was a bad idea.

But what he'd said. What he'd said made so much sense, and it would only have made sense if he was someone like her. If he also saw visions that led him to—what? What else might one do if not solving crimes? Laura had chosen a life path that allowed her to put her visions to work, but what would she have done with them if law enforcement hadn't been an option?

What would a civilian do with visions of the future?

She'd all but given up on finding someone like her a while ago. Every lead had been a dead end. Every hint had turned out to be just a fraud or someone with mental problems. Or coincidence. Someone dreaming and then a similar event randomly happening later, not true visions. She'd scoured message boards, pored over historical papers and archives, researched everything possible on the topic of psychics, and never before had she managed to find a single human soul in the history of existence who could actually do what she could do.

Laura had responsibilities as a mother. But she'd been wondering for so long. She'd been alone for so long. Desperate for someone, anyone, who could tell her how these visions really worked, how to control them, how to know what they meant without always feeling shaken and confused.

She could suggest they go elsewhere, but she couldn't leave Lacey on her own, even in the middle of the night. If she woke up needing her mother... no, she couldn't go for a walk or a coffee with him. There was the option of telling him to come back tomorrow, but it didn't feel as though that was going to be a real choice either. There was something surreal about this meeting. Like it could only have happened under moonlight.

This man might be dangerous. But she was a special agent. She was dangerous in her own right, and he was an old man. Not as strong, not as fast, not as durable as she was.

And he might have the answers that she needed.

Laura stepped to one side. "Come in," she said, because she needed to know.

NOW AVAILABLE!

ALREADY CHOSEN
(A Laura Frost FBI Suspense Thriller—Book 7)

Women are turning up dead, a creepy and inexplicable mannequin found at each crime scene beside them. As FBI Special Agent Laura Frost races to decode this serial killer's signature, her conflicting visions are leading her astray. Has she lost her gift?

"A masterpiece of thriller and mystery."
—Books and Movie Reviews, Roberto Mattos (re Once Gone)

ALREADY CHOSEN (A Laura Frost FBI Suspense Thriller) is book #7 in a long-anticipated new series by #1 bestseller and USA Today bestselling author Blake Pierce, whose bestseller Once Gone (a free download) has received over 1,000 five star reviews. The Laura Frost series begins with ALREADY GONE (Book #1).

FBI Special Agent and single mom Laura Frost, 35, is haunted by her talent: a psychic ability which she refuses to face and which she keeps secret from her colleagues. While Laura gets obscured glimpses of what the killer may do next, she must decide whether to trust her confusing gift—or her investigative work.

As Laura inspects the mannequins, holding hands with the victims, she can feel the answer to the killer's riddle right out of reach. What is he hinting at?

The only solution is to enter his dark mind, to play his game.

But then, there may be no way out.

A page-turning and harrowing crime thriller featuring a brilliant and tortured FBI agent, the LAURA FROST series is a startlingly fresh mystery, rife with suspense, twists and turns, shocking revelations, and driven by a breakneck pace that will keep you flipping pages late into the night.

Books #8 and #9 in the series—ALREADY LOST and ALREADY HIS—are now also available.

"An edge of your seat thriller in a new series that keeps you turning pages! ...So many twists, turns and red herrings... I can't wait to see what happens next."
—Reader review (*Her Last Wish*)

"A strong, complex story about two FBI agents trying to stop a serial killer. If you want an author to capture your attention and have you guessing, yet trying to put the pieces together, Pierce is your author!"
—Reader review (*Her Last Wish*)

"A typical Blake Pierce twisting, turning, roller coaster ride suspense thriller. Will have you turning the pages to the last sentence of the last chapter!!!"
—Reader review (*City of Prey*)

"Right from the start we have an unusual protagonist that I haven't seen done in this genre before. The action is nonstop... A very atmospheric novel that will keep you turning pages well into the wee hours."
—Reader review (*City of Prey*)

"Everything that I look for in a book... a great plot, interesting characters, and grabs your interest right away. The book moves along at a breakneck pace and stays that way until the end. Now on go I to book two!"
—Reader review (*Girl, Alone*)

"Exciting, heart pounding, edge of your seat book... a must read for mystery and suspense readers!"
—Reader review (*Girl, Alone*)

Blake Pierce

Blake Pierce is the USA Today bestselling author of the RILEY PAGE mystery series, which includes seventeen books. Blake Pierce is also the author of the MACKENZIE WHITE mystery series, comprising fourteen books; of the AVERY BLACK mystery series, comprising six books; of the KERI LOCKE mystery series, comprising five books; of the MAKING OF RILEY PAIGE mystery series, comprising six books; of the KATE WISE mystery series, comprising seven books; of the CHLOE FINE psychological suspense mystery, comprising six books; of the JESSE HUNT psychological suspense thriller series, comprising twenty four books; of the AU PAIR psychological suspense thriller series, comprising three books; of the ZOE PRIME mystery series, comprising six books; of the ADELE SHARP mystery series, comprising fifteen books, of the EUROPEAN VOYAGE cozy mystery series, comprising four books; of the new LAURA FROST FBI suspense thriller, comprising nine books (and counting); of the new ELLA DARK FBI suspense thriller, comprising eleven books (and counting); of the A YEAR IN EUROPE cozy mystery series, comprising nine books, of the AVA GOLD mystery series, comprising six books (and counting); of the RACHEL GIFT mystery series, comprising six books (and counting); of the VALERIE LAW mystery series, comprising six books (and counting); and of the PAIGE KING mystery series, comprising six books (and counting).

An avid reader and lifelong fan of the mystery and thriller genres, Blake loves to hear from you, so please feel free to visit www.blakepierceauthor.com to learn more and stay in touch.

BOOKS BY BLAKE PIERCE

PAIGE KING MYSTERY SERIES
THE GIRL HE PINED (Book #1)
THE GIRL HE CHOSE (Book #2)
THE GIRL HE TOOK (Book #3)
THE GIRL HE WISHED (Book #4)
THE GIRL HE CROWNED (Book #5)
THE GIRL HE WATCHED (Book #6)

VALERIE LAW MYSTERY SERIES
NO MERCY (Book #1)
NO PITY (Book #2)
NO FEAR (Book #3)
NO SLEEP (Book #4)
NO QUARTER (Book #5)
NO CHANCE (Book #6)

RACHEL GIFT MYSTERY SERIES
HER LAST WISH (Book #1)
HER LAST CHANCE (Book #2)
HER LAST HOPE (Book #3)
HER LAST FEAR (Book #4)
HER LAST CHOICE (Book #5)
HER LAST BREATH (Book #6)

AVA GOLD MYSTERY SERIES
CITY OF PREY (Book #1)
CITY OF FEAR (Book #2)
CITY OF BONES (Book #3)
CITY OF GHOSTS (Book #4)
CITY OF DEATH (Book #5)
CITY OF VICE (Book #6)

A YEAR IN EUROPE
A MURDER IN PARIS (Book #1)
DEATH IN FLORENCE (Book #2)
VENGEANCE IN VIENNA (Book #3)

A FATALITY IN SPAIN (Book #4)

ELLA DARK FBI SUSPENSE THRILLER
GIRL, ALONE (Book #1)
GIRL, TAKEN (Book #2)
GIRL, HUNTED (Book #3)
GIRL, SILENCED (Book #4)
GIRL, VANISHED (Book 5)
GIRL ERASED (Book #6)
GIRL, FORSAKEN (Book #7)
GIRL, TRAPPED (Book #8)
GIRL, EXPENDABLE (Book #9)
GIRL, ESCAPED (Book #10)
GIRL, HIS (Book #11)

LAURA FROST FBI SUSPENSE THRILLER
ALREADY GONE (Book #1)
ALREADY SEEN (Book #2)
ALREADY TRAPPED (Book #3)
ALREADY MISSING (Book #4)
ALREADY DEAD (Book #5)
ALREADY TAKEN (Book #6)
ALREADY CHOSEN (Book #7)
ALREADY LOST (Book #8)
ALREADY HIS (Book #9)

EUROPEAN VOYAGE COZY MYSTERY SERIES
MURDER (AND BAKLAVA) (Book #1)
DEATH (AND APPLE STRUDEL) (Book #2)
CRIME (AND LAGER) (Book #3)
MISFORTUNE (AND GOUDA) (Book #4)
CALAMITY (AND A DANISH) (Book #5)
MAYHEM (AND HERRING) (Book #6)

ADELE SHARP MYSTERY SERIES
LEFT TO DIE (Book #1)
LEFT TO RUN (Book #2)
LEFT TO HIDE (Book #3)
LEFT TO KILL (Book #4)
LEFT TO MURDER (Book #5)

LEFT TO ENVY (Book #6)
LEFT TO LAPSE (Book #7)
LEFT TO VANISH (Book #8)
LEFT TO HUNT (Book #9)
LEFT TO FEAR (Book #10)
LEFT TO PREY (Book #11)
LEFT TO LURE (Book #12)
LEFT TO CRAVE (Book #13)
LEFT TO LOATHE (Book #14)
LEFT TO HARM (Book #15)

THE AU PAIR SERIES
ALMOST GONE (Book#1)
ALMOST LOST (Book #2)
ALMOST DEAD (Book #3)

ZOE PRIME MYSTERY SERIES
FACE OF DEATH (Book#1)
FACE OF MURDER (Book #2)
FACE OF FEAR (Book #3)
FACE OF MADNESS (Book #4)
FACE OF FURY (Book #5)
FACE OF DARKNESS (Book #6)

A JESSIE HUNT PSYCHOLOGICAL SUSPENSE SERIES
THE PERFECT WIFE (Book #1)
THE PERFECT BLOCK (Book #2)
THE PERFECT HOUSE (Book #3)
THE PERFECT SMILE (Book #4)
THE PERFECT LIE (Book #5)
THE PERFECT LOOK (Book #6)
THE PERFECT AFFAIR (Book #7)
THE PERFECT ALIBI (Book #8)
THE PERFECT NEIGHBOR (Book #9)
THE PERFECT DISGUISE (Book #10)
THE PERFECT SECRET (Book #11)
THE PERFECT FAÇADE (Book #12)
THE PERFECT IMPRESSION (Book #13)
THE PERFECT DECEIT (Book #14)
THE PERFECT MISTRESS (Book #15)

THE PERFECT IMAGE (Book #16)
THE PERFECT VEIL (Book #17)
THE PERFECT INDISCRETION (Book #18)
THE PERFECT RUMOR (Book #19)
THE PERFECT COUPLE (Book #20)
THE PERFECT MURDER (Book #21)
THE PERFECT HUSBAND (Book #22)
THE PERFECT SCANDAL (Book #23)
THE PERFECT MASK (Book #24)

CHLOE FINE PSYCHOLOGICAL SUSPENSE SERIES
NEXT DOOR (Book #1)
A NEIGHBOR'S LIE (Book #2)
CUL DE SAC (Book #3)
SILENT NEIGHBOR (Book #4)
HOMECOMING (Book #5)
TINTED WINDOWS (Book #6)

KATE WISE MYSTERY SERIES
IF SHE KNEW (Book #1)
IF SHE SAW (Book #2)
IF SHE RAN (Book #3)
IF SHE HID (Book #4)
IF SHE FLED (Book #5)
IF SHE FEARED (Book #6)
IF SHE HEARD (Book #7)

THE MAKING OF RILEY PAIGE SERIES
WATCHING (Book #1)
WAITING (Book #2)
LURING (Book #3)
TAKING (Book #4)
STALKING (Book #5)
KILLING (Book #6)

RILEY PAIGE MYSTERY SERIES
ONCE GONE (Book #1)
ONCE TAKEN (Book #2)
ONCE CRAVED (Book #3)

ONCE LURED (Book #4)
ONCE HUNTED (Book #5)
ONCE PINED (Book #6)
ONCE FORSAKEN (Book #7)
ONCE COLD (Book #8)
ONCE STALKED (Book #9)
ONCE LOST (Book #10)
ONCE BURIED (Book #11)
ONCE BOUND (Book #12)
ONCE TRAPPED (Book #13)
ONCE DORMANT (Book #14)
ONCE SHUNNED (Book #15)
ONCE MISSED (Book #16)
ONCE CHOSEN (Book #17)

MACKENZIE WHITE MYSTERY SERIES
BEFORE HE KILLS (Book #1)
BEFORE HE SEES (Book #2)
BEFORE HE COVETS (Book #3)
BEFORE HE TAKES (Book #4)
BEFORE HE NEEDS (Book #5)
BEFORE HE FEELS (Book #6)
BEFORE HE SINS (Book #7)
BEFORE HE HUNTS (Book #8)
BEFORE HE PREYS (Book #9)
BEFORE HE LONGS (Book #10)
BEFORE HE LAPSES (Book #11)
BEFORE HE ENVIES (Book #12)
BEFORE HE STALKS (Book #13)
BEFORE HE HARMS (Book #14)

AVERY BLACK MYSTERY SERIES
CAUSE TO KILL (Book #1)
CAUSE TO RUN (Book #2)
CAUSE TO HIDE (Book #3)
CAUSE TO FEAR (Book #4)
CAUSE TO SAVE (Book #5)
CAUSE TO DREAD (Book #6)

KERI LOCKE MYSTERY SERIES

Made in the USA
Las Vegas, NV
17 December 2022

63209586R00105